48 and Counting
A Story of Money, Love and Bicycling

Jonathan Clements

ISBN: 1478392134
ISBN-13: 978-1478392132

For Hannah and Henry

CONTENTS

ACKNOWLEDGMENTS

Many thanks to Julia Bass, Hannah Clements, Henry Clements, Victoria Clements, June Dosik, Ben Eyler, Roxanne Goble, David Hamilton, Ross Levin, Michelle Maghribi, Linda Schaffer-Gutman and David Sheehan, who were all kind enough either to read the manuscript before publication or comment on the cover design, and sometimes both. I appreciated your many suggestions and, as you'll discover, took many of them. What about the suggestions I didn't take? My bad.

The cover reproduces part of Henri de Toulouse-Lautrec's 1896 poster, *La Chaine Simpson*. Merci beaucoup, Henri.

This book is for Hannah and Henry. I consider myself a lucky person—but never luckier than when I think of my two glorious children, who forever astonish me with their accomplishments, their fierce intelligence and their compassion.

SPRING

He stared at his father's old aluminum bicycle. It had sat there unused for two years, ever since he had carted it home after his father's death. Why had he taken it? It had no real value. The chain was rusted, the faux leather seat was cracked and brown spots speckled the frame.

But his father had cherished the bike, so for Max it offered a last chance at intimacy. It was the same reason he had taken his father's sandals, some of his ties and a handful of his ratty old T-shirts. They had been part of his father, triggering memories of his face and prompting Max to whisper once again, "Hey Dad, how are you? It's me, Max. Yeah, I'm still here. I'm still thinking about you."

Max didn't really think his father was there. He had no fanciful notions of heaven, angels or any of that nonsense. But he felt something of his father was there in the bike, a small trace of immortality. He recalled the graceful way his father would dismount. As the bike slowed, he would stand on the left pedal and swing his right leg over the seat and back tire, so both legs were on the same side of the bike as he glided to a halt. Even as he grew older and more arthritic, his father could perform that neat trick.

Max pulled the bicycle from the garage and leant it against the garden fence. It was late March and this was supposed to be spring cleaning. He had already tossed out a bent garden fork, a leaking hose and some old paint cans. But this was one item he couldn't part with.

The tires were flat, so he found a pump and filled them with air. He dug up a can of oil and dripped it on the chain, and then lifted the back wheel and gave the pedals a spin. The chain and cogs uttered a low whir. Max found himself smiling at the almost-forgotten ritual. Was he recalling helping his kids with their bikes—or was he remembering his own childhood?

He slung his leg over the seat, pushed off with his left foot, drove down the pedal with his right and headed out into the Sunday morning traffic.

"That's nice, dear." Karen didn't mean to sound patronizing. In fact, she didn't mean to convey anything at all, except the sense that she was listening, which she wasn't.

Max stood in the kitchen, patches of sweat under either arm, his face slightly flushed. "No, really, it felt so cool," he repeated again, trying to impart the pleasure of pedaling for half an hour around the suburban neighborhood of me-too homes. "It was like being a little kid again. The brakes seem a little off and I'm having trouble getting the gears to shift. But there's something totally cool about it."

Karen smiled her meaningless smile and Max shook his head slowly, marveling at the death of passion. He grabbed a cup of coffee and headed to the second-floor bathroom, noting once again the irritating groan emanating from the staircase's eighth step. Would it give out one day when he or Karen was standing on it, sending one of them plummeting to the basement?

"We were college sweethearts." It was their signature four-word headline used whenever meeting new acquaintances. The emphasis had always been on the fourth word. Had it shifted to the second? He had spotted Karen in a statistics class during their sophomore year. At the next lecture, he snagged the seat next to her. The weeks that followed were a whirlwind of playful conversations, lustful kisses and hungry, ham-fisted lovemaking. Today, he could still vaguely remember the sequence of events, but the lust and the hunger were just labels he associated with those days, not feelings he could actually recall.

A year after they graduated, he married a sassy, wisecracking lover. A quarter century later, he resided with a studiously disinterested roommate. How the fuck had that happened? Let's face it, they weren't a pretty sight. They liked to think they had reached their late 40s looking a little less worn than their friends. But her hips had spread and his belly protruded. Dear God, even his butt looked a little big. A guy with a big butt? That was just sad. He never thought of himself as handsome, but imagined he was on the better side of average. It was a sign of trouble, however, that he was now pickier about his clothes. Teenagers could wear rags and look mesmerizing. But as Max had aged, he had taken to covering his increasingly lumpy body with designer labels.

He showered and, still wet, kissed Karen wearing just a towel, hoping to get lucky. He wasn't. So he stuffed his fading erection into a pair of jeans and sought solace in his study, looking at his financial accounts online.

He found the balances comforting. He and Karen had seen friends struggle. Marriages had fallen apart, children had developed emotional problems, jobs had been lost, major financial mistakes had been made. But that wasn't him and Karen. For 25 years, they had kept their heads down, barreled forward and collected the trophies that came with financial success.

They had a comfortable, mortgage-free home in central New Jersey. They had a portfolio that was worth almost $3 million. He had an undemanding job that paid him a handsome income. They had two reasonably well-adjusted daughters, one in college in Chicago, the other already graduated and working in Boston.

And yet his life sucked. Okay, sucked was too strong a word. He didn't think his expectations were all that high. Nonetheless, he couldn't escape the sense of disappointment. He had more worldly success than he could reasonably have hoped for, but happiness eluded him. He was undoubtedly less happy than when he was a penniless college student or when he and Karen were first building a life together and their finances teetered on the cusp of insolvency. He suspected he was even less happy than he was just a few years ago. Whatever money had bought him, it wasn't joy or even a mild sense of contentment.

It was tempting to blame Karen. She was missing in action and had been for years. As Clare and Melanie had romped through high school, picking up self-confidence and losing interest in home life, Karen had grown increasingly agitated. But then things got busy in human resources—layoffs were in the works—and they asked her to go from part-time to full-time. Dispensing misery became Karen's passion. Nobody could fire an employee with her panache. She had turned empathy into an art form. Laid-off employees left feeling that HR was truly their friend. Karen was fulfilled.

Max was horny. When Karen announced she was off to the mall, he waited for the sound of the departing car and then headed to the bathroom to masturbate.

The phone rang. Max picked up the receiver awkwardly with his left hand while examining his right, wondering whether he had got it totally clean.

"Hello?"

"Hey, Dad."

"Clare, how are things?"

Max endeavored to talk to both his daughters at least once a week. Clare, the oldest, always called. Melanie? He almost always had to call her.

Max assumed the role of father figure, asking Clare about her job, her new apartment and her evenings out. She was working in a downtown Boston hospital as a staff assistant in the chief executive's office, with aspirations to rise through the administrative ranks. It was a lot of menial work and late hours, but the job held promise and she attacked the work week with a zeal Max vaguely recalled from his 20s.

He wondered what his daughter would think if she had just seen him in the bathroom. Everybody had secret lives. They took drugs, had affairs, struggled with alcohol, shopped compulsively, had strange sexual peccadilloes. By contrast, Max's secret life was really pretty dull. Still, he winced at the thought of his daughter bursting into the bathroom and catching him. He gave his head a vigorous shake, as though trying to dislodge the image from his mind.

Max had thought his little money-management business would be his life's big achievement. But lately, it didn't seem all that big or all that much of an achievement. As he came to realize he would leave the most modest of marks on the world, he found himself increasingly invested in his daughters' success, especially Clare's. He knew he shouldn't play favorites, but he always felt a special bond with her.

He wanted so much to see her succeed, without knowing precisely why. Maybe it was just parental pride in his daughter's accomplishments. Maybe he figured success would make her happy, even though it hadn't done much for him. Maybe it was the hope that she would bring glory to the family name—though, let's face it, she would probably marry some chauvinistic egomaniac and his future son-in-law would insist Clare change her surname.

Most of their weekly conversation was Clare talking and Max listening. He wasn't sure her life was any more exciting than his. But she was certainly more excited by it.

"So what have you been up to, Dad?" That was usually the signal that they were in the conversation's closing minutes.

"Not a whole lot. Cleaned the carburetor on the lawn mower, so it's ready for the new season. Picked up some of the twigs and branches that came down over the winter. Also cleaned out the garage. Remember Grandpa's bike?"

"Are we about to talk about your midlife crisis again?"

"Dear God, you're a cruel child."

"And that's why you love me. So go on, finish what you were saying."

"I saw the bike sitting in the garage, covered with dust and cobwebs. I felt badly, like I'd been neglecting it, so I pumped up the tires and took it for a spin."

"You got some exercise?" Clare had been bugging both him and Karen to start working out.

"My body will probably be screaming tomorrow morning. I'll be sure to blame you."

"Did you think about Grandpa when you were riding?"

"Yeah, I thought about him a lot," said Max. "I thought about how I was sitting on the same saddle he used to sit on. I think he would have been happy to see the old bike out on the road again. I think I'm going to take it out more often."

"But Jerry says gold is at the start of a multi-year bull market?"

Who the hell was Jerry? Max didn't want to drag out the conversation, so he didn't ask.

"Gold has been in a multi-year bull market for the past decade," he pointed out, shifting silently in his seat, searching for the least uncomfortable position for his aching back. "The time to buy gold was ten years ago, when it was at a fraction of today's price."

"So the rally will continue?" asked Mrs. Deveney hopefully.

"I have no idea," allowed Max, stretching out his legs beneath the desk, trying to stop them from seizing up. Maybe riding two days in a row wasn't so smart. "But I do know that every increase in price effectively steals gains from the future. Because of the big gains of the past ten years, we should be less enthusiastic, not more so."

Clients either got it or they didn't—and most didn't. They couldn't accept that the future was unknowable and the past was a rotten guide to what lay ahead. They were betting their financial future. Chaos might be the reality, but it was emotionally unacceptable. So they assumed the future could be divined and that Max had the inside scoop.

Max vigorously denied any prescience. He would joke that "stock-market forecasters exist to make astrologers look good." He repeatedly explained that the performance of markets couldn't be predicted and that, instead, his job was to manage the amount of risk clients took, the tax bill generated by their investments, and each portfolio's trading costs and fund expenses. But most clients weren't buying it: They took Max's assertion that he was no clairvoyant as false modesty and assured themselves he knew more than he was letting on.

"So we won't be buying gold?"

"Not today, Mrs. Deveney. You're in wonderful financial shape. There's no need to take a risk like that."

"Such a shame. It seems like such an exciting

investment."

"Yes, I'm sure it would be," said Max, trying hard not to grimace as his back offered further protests. "I've been meaning to ask: How's David? Last time, you were saying his massage business is really taking off. You must be very proud."

In truth, Max didn't just manage a portfolio's risk, costs and taxes. He also managed clients. In fact, that was how he spent most of his time.

It was a day full of surprises—Max could never be sure what issues or worries clients would raise next—and yet there was a comforting predictability to it all. However insistent or irritating a client was, Max knew the meeting would be over in an hour and soon he would be starting afresh with a new client. If only he could escape conversations with Karen so easily. Max sighed silently to himself as Mrs. Deveney continued to prattle.

There was also a comforting predictability to the advice he had to deliver. Rein in excessive enthusiasm, as he was with Mrs. Deveney today. Keep clients invested when they were unnerved by plunging markets. Make sure they saved enough, didn't go overboard on debt, bought the right insurance and had an estate plan.

To get clients to do all of this, he would listen—and let them tell their story, endless chatter about their jobs, their childhood, their financial dreams. Max would take copious notes, so he could replay the information at subsequent meetings, as if he were an attentive friend who always remembered the fascinating things they said. He would throw in occasional questions, getting clients to flesh out why they wanted the larger house and what they would do with their retirement.

But mostly, he would ask about family. It was almost sickeningly manipulative. Ask about the parents, the kids, the grandkids, and clients would light up and go into verbal overdrive. The details came pouring out, the dreams, the disappointments, the worries. Along the way, something magical happened: Max became part of the family. For younger clients, he was the wise uncle. For middle-aged clients, he was the savvy cousin. For elderly clients, he was the clever son-in-law. He was the smart family member who was always happy to hear from them, always cheerful on the phone and in person, who understood them, and whom they could call at any time for guidance and reassurance.

They just happened to be paying one percent a year for the privilege. The math was embarrassingly favorable to Max. Whitfield Financial Advisors was tiny by Wall Street standards, with just $70 million of clients' money under management. The one percent a year on $70 million worked out to $700,000 in revenue. His office space and staff, which consisted of one full-time and one part-time employee, coupled with accounting and legal expenses, cost him $350,000.

That left $350,000 for Max. He was used to it now, almost took it for granted. But early on, when the money started gushing in, he could hardly believe his good fortune. Who knew how much was pocketed by other advisors, some of whom managed $1 billion and more?

Max stood stiff-legged by his office door. "Alison,

could you show Mrs. Deveney out?"

"Of course, Mr. Whitfield. Come this way, Mrs. Deveney. How are you? How's David?"

Alison only called him Mr. Whitfield when clients were around. She thought it made Max seem more authoritative and the office more professional, and he never suggested she change. She suspected Max liked it.

In fact, Alison suspected he liked her. She knew she was a little on the heavy side. But she felt she carried the extra pounds well, that they accentuated her curves and made her breasts fuller. The weight, which might have made an older woman appear dowdy, added to her voluptuousness and allowed her to project an image of someone who was mature yet fun.

She knew Max noticed her. She felt his glance linger on her as she left the room, just as she saw his glance linger on other women. It was as though they were nature's puppets: If she felt he was flirting with her, Alison would respond by flaunting it just a little. She doubted he would ever actually try anything and, if he did, she wasn't sure how she would react. Probably she would laugh it off, playfully slap his face and call him a dirty old man. Mostly, she felt a little sorry for him, even though he was her boss and 20 years her senior.

"How about we set up your next quarterly meeting for late June? Would that be okay, Mrs. Deveney?"

"That would be fine, dear."

"I'll put you down for June 28 at 11 a.m. and, as usual, I'll phone a few days before with a reminder. Thanks so much for coming in. It's been great to see you. Enjoy the warmer weather."

Alison had been hired by Max six years earlier, when she was a newly minted college graduate. She had slowly made herself indispensible, so now the only other employee was a part-time bookkeeper who worked from home. She had learned the computer systems, read the finance books Max recommended, passed the necessary exams to obtain her securities licenses and was just a year away from earning her Certified Financial Planner designation. She had a knack for the business. She knew it and Max did, too. Every so often, when she felt in need of a pay raise or a loftier title, she would mutter about moving on. The extra money and a new title would quickly follow, though her duties changed only slowly. Still, she reckoned she was on course to be Max's successor and observed him like an eager anthropologist.

It was just scraps of evidence, really, but together the scraps added up. He was arriving at the office a little later. He was slower to call back clients and quicker to disparage their investment acumen. He was less likely to ask clients if they had friends or family members who needed his services. He was slower to press his business card into the hands of new acquaintances. He was less eager to upgrade the office software and he no longer bothered with financial-planning conferences. On the phone, he was more impatient with his wife. Just this morning, he was waxing eloquent about his father's old bicycle but didn't bother asking which clients had appointments that day. His grip on the things he used to care about was starting to loosen.

Alison had seen the transformation in the time she had worked for him, with much of the change coming during the past few years. To her, it seemed like Max had decided he had sacrificed too much for the sake of his family and his business. He was playing faster and looser with the world he had so carefully constructed for himself, as he tried to figure out how little sacrificing he could get away with. Alison often found herself cleaning up the resulting mess, calling back the clients he hadn't called and chatting with them in the reception area because he was late getting back from lunch.

She didn't mind: She figured it made her more indispensible and she would get her reward, that eventually she would own Whitfield Financial Advisors. Max had never discussed the business's future with her. He tended to be tight-lipped about the firm's finances. But he had signaled his intentions by recently giving her a small stake in Whitfield Financial.

She found watching Max fascinating, in the way it's fascinating to watch a car accident slowly unfurl. She wasn't sure how big a smash it would be. But she increasingly sensed that there would indeed be a crash. Would Max damage the business she one day hoped to run? Alison sat at her desk and toyed with the question.

He turned away from the counter, sandwich and bag of potato chips in hand, and she immediately caught his eye. She had a small birthmark just above her lip that complemented her brown eyes and hair. To some, it might have been a blemish. But to Max, it took a pretty face and made it beautiful by offering a poignant declaration of character.

Of course, many women caught Max's eye. That

had always been the case. He enjoyed looking at women, those who passed him on the street, his female clients, Alison, pretty much anybody of the opposite sex who was moderately attractive. But he sensed that lately he was looking more intently, that he was no longer a casual observer. He wondered whether he was turning into a letch, an aging pervert who stares at women with that look of unabashed sexual interest and not the slightest chance of success.

"Good book?" he asked.

For Christ's sake, who was he becoming? Now, he wasn't just leering at women, he was trying to engage them in conversation. He never did that.

She looked startled.

"It's really much too good a book for a place like this," Max persisted, suddenly fearful he was making a fool of himself. "Something trashier would fit the ambience better. If the guys behind the counter catch you, you may be barred forever from this fine eating establishment."

She laughed. "I'm not a big reader of trashy novels."

"You should try them. You wouldn't appear nearly so intimidating to the weirdoes who accost you in Italian delicatessens."

She laughed again, an easy laugh that made her eyes light up. Max was smitten. This woman with the birthmark above her lip was more than just strikingly beautiful. He felt a chemistry with her, an instantaneous attraction that couldn't be explained by appearance alone. Were his hormones that out of control? He wondered.

"So, do you often accost women in delicatessens?"

"Actually, this is the first time," Max confided.

14

"Seriously. Never done it before. But I couldn't help myself."

"Really?" she said. "Is that flattery or a confession? Maybe it's step three in the weirdoes' 12-step program."

"Maybe." It was Max's turn to laugh. "Or maybe it's step five. I can't remember. Truth is, you never know what weird things we weirdoes might say. Anyway, didn't mean to interrupt your lunch. Enjoy your book. I'm Max, by the way. Hope to see you around."

He grinned and made his escape. He wasn't quite sure what he had done, but he had done it. Max felt triumphant.

He stood up on the pedals as the small hill began to bite and immediately felt the burning in his quads. Max quickly sat down, sensed the bike was slowing alarmingly, desperately played with the gears and eventually managed to downshift. The easier gear at his disposal, he spun like crazy and clambered the slope, a jarring contrast of imperceptible forward motion and furiously fast pedaling.

It was his fourth time up the small hill. His breath came in short gasps and spit hung from his chin. The hands of his wrist watch suggested he had been out for 47 minutes. He had hoped to make an hour, but he was done. He eased off the pedals, coasted a little and, for the first time during the ride, noticed the dew on the neighborhood lawns and the way it sparkled in the morning sun. He briefly soaked up the view before turning for home, craving coffee.

Max closed the bathroom door and studied his

naked self in the mirror. His belly still bulged. His arms looked white and fleshy. His hair, mostly black but with a smattering of gray, was slathered to his head by dried sweat. His penis, battered by the bicycle seat, had sounded the retreat. Nonetheless, he felt good, like his body had been used in a way it hadn't been used in a long time. He could feel his muscles fighting to adjust. He had now bicycled six times in the last 11 days. The pain in his legs was slowly fading and a new sense of strength was replacing it.

"Are you okay?" Karen asked as he walked into the kitchen, showered and dressed for work.

"I went out on the bike again."

"I know. I saw you leave. You look red."

"I haven't cooled down from the ride."

Karen appeared doubtful. "Don't give yourself a heart attack."

"This is the look of a man on the road back to fitness and youth, and you're the beneficiary. Soon, you'll be sleeping with a far younger man."

Karen looked like she could hardly have cared less. "Remember, I've got to give a presentation in Manhattan today."

Max hadn't remembered. For the first time during the conversation, he focused on her. She looked good, her skirt reaching the top of her knees and the legs below suggesting there was even better above. Max realized it had been a long time since he had noticed anything about his wife's appearance. Did she always get this dressed up for work or was this a special outfit for today? He couldn't recall seeing the skirt before. It seemed like something Alison might wear. Was Karen trying to look younger?

"At the big employee relations expo," she prodded

him. "I'm speaking in the afternoon. About the latest headcount reduction techniques."

"Right," said Max, still not sure he remembered.

"I'll be home late. There's plenty of stuff in the refrigerator."

"Right," said Max again, his attention wandering to the day ahead.

He arrived 18 minutes late, noted Alison. He thought a client would be waiting. No clients were. Alison was trying to work around Max's new tardiness. Her latest strategy: She was scheduling client meetings for 30 minutes later than Max expected them.

"You got lucky," chided Alison, frowning with disapproval. "Mr. Cameron is late."

"Yes, yes, lucky indeed," grumbled Max, who had a vague sense that recently many clients were arriving late and yet none ever apologized. But this stray thought flitted away as he caught sight of Alison's breasts outlined beneath her shirt. He was definitely becoming a letch, maybe even a budding sexual predator.

"My face is up here," she wanted to say, as it became clear Max was checking her out. But instead she said, "I think Mr. Cameron is interested in gold. He asked me about it when I phoned yesterday to confirm his appointment."

"Sweet Jesus," despaired Max, shaking his head and forgetting about Alison's breasts. "Not fucking gold again."

"You shouldn't be surprised clients are asking about it. Every time you turn on the radio or TV, it's the only thing the financial commentators are talking about."

"They're idiots. Don't they realize gold was at $250 a decade ago? It's a little late in the day to be buying."

"Even my parents are talking about it and their idea of excitement is a five-year certificate of deposit."

"I just don't get it," Max said. "I can understand being a little more or less excited. But it's like somebody flips a switch and the herd mentality kicks in. We start goading each other to invest with silly stories about why the price is going up and up and up."

"Do you know gold climbed $100 over the past week? Yesterday, it broke $1,500."

"Which is another reason not to buy it," said Max, growing increasingly agitated. "I have no clue what gold is worth. It doesn't earn a profit or pay a dividend. It's useless except as jewelry. It's worth whatever we collectively think it's worth, which could be $300 an ounce or $3,000. I'd much rather stick with stocks and bonds any time. At least you have some idea what their value is."

"But everybody's asking about gold," said Alison, sounding like a seven-year-old pleading for a new doll. "If we don't start adding it to portfolios, we're going to lose clients."

"Well, they aren't getting it. They can all fuck themselves."

As Max banged his office door closed, he realized his final pronouncement was perhaps overly dramatic. He hoped it wouldn't end up costing him another pay raise for Alison.

*

He was captivated by the rows of gorgeous bicycles, even though he hadn't a clue what he was looking at. Max wasn't much of a shopper. He detested the crowds and the brazen appeal to humankind's baser instincts—vanity, greed, envy, a hankering for status.

Still, over the years, he had managed to spend hundreds of thousands of dollars, maybe even millions. Who knew how much he had parted with? He had bought the flat-screen television, the antique roll-top desk, the luxury sedan, each time sure that the new purchase would somehow transform his life and bring him immense joy. But he wasn't sure the flat-screen television was really a big improvement. He didn't even notice the antique desk anymore. The luxury sedan quickly became just another way to get around town and then, when the built-in navigation system malfunctioned, it became a way to get around town accompanied by the crazed ranting of the hopelessly confused GPS lady. Possessions, by themselves, didn't seem to have brought him much more than an initial, fleeting pleasure.

But maybe a new bicycle would be different. He was entranced by the lines of each frame, many ramrod straight, others gently curved. He delighted in the glistening colors, some bikes sparkling red, some neon green, some electric blue. It was as though folks threw out all restraint when it came to bicycles and embraced colors they would never ordinarily associate with. He stood in his grey suit and loosened his tie.

"Can I help you?"

This, Max realized, was not the time to be the guy who never asked for directions. "Absolutely," he confessed. "I want to buy a new bicycle and I haven't the slightest idea how one bike differs from the next."

"What sort of riding do you do?"

Max felt the young sales clerk was sizing him up, eyeing his soft hands, slightly pudgy face, protruding stomach. "I've been riding my Dad's old bike," he began, sensing that—if he was to be matched with the right bicycle—the kid needed to know his story. "I'm up to almost an hour. But the gears don't always shift and the bike's heavy. I thought about getting it fixed. But I want to ride farther and faster, and I don't think I can do that on the old bike."

It was as close to dreaming out loud as Max would allow himself. He believed he could ride a hell of a lot farther and a hell of a lot faster. As he rode around the suburban streets, he told himself tales of out climbing other riders, beating them in the sprint and winning races. Something about cycling had kidnapped his imagination and was holding it hostage. He felt that maybe, just maybe, he could be really good at this bicycling thing.

"So you want to ride on roads, not trails?"

"Right."

"How much are you looking to spend?"

"How much do I need to spend?"

"If people are starting out and they're pretty serious, I usually encourage them to spend $1,500 or so. That'll get you a decent road bike with a mostly aluminum frame but with some carbon and you'll get okay components."

"But you could spend more?"

"Oh yeah, a lot more."

Ninety minutes—and two missed client meetings—later, Max walked out with a $5,400 bicycle, special bicycling shoes that clipped into the pedals, a bike computer, two pairs of spandex shorts, two riding jerseys, helmet, gloves and a bag full of other paraphernalia. He was $6,500 poorer and felt like a kid at Christmas.

"You spent $6,500?" They were standing either side of the kitchen table, both clasping coffee cups and halfway dressed for the office. Max was wearing a shirt, tie and black socks, but no trousers. Karen was in a bra and skirt, but hadn't yet settled on a blouse. After 25 years together, they weren't oblivious to each other's partial nakedness, but it didn't stir more than a passing interest.

Max was a little sheepish about his spending spree. As his business had prospered and Karen had started collecting a full-time salary, they had let their standard of living drift higher. Even so, they spent far less than they earned and rarely made a major purchase without consulting each other.

But Max was also secretly pleased with himself. He had finally managed to do something that snapped Karen out of her self-absorbed reverie. When had either of them last done more than recite their day's schedule in the morning and recount the day's events in the evening? When had they last had a profound conversation, let alone a good fight?

"The $6,500 includes the pedals and shoes and a bunch of other gear," he offered, hoping to provoke another outburst.

"Are you having a midlife crisis?"

Probably, thought Max. I'm also turning into a sexual pervert and I've taken to speaking to strange women with birthmarks above their lips. But these didn't seem like the sorts of things he should admit to, so he went for the diversion. "How was yesterday's presentation?"

"The presentation?" Karen seemed surprised by the question, but she quickly collected herself. "I didn't think you'd be interested or I would have told you all about it. It went really well. Lots of questions from the audience. Lots of interest in headcount reduction. Looks like business will be booming over the next 12 months."

"That's wonderful, honey," said Max, who thought it anything but.

"Yes, I was talking to our director of human resources and he says we've got some tough second-quarter numbers to hit. You know how busy it gets when we have these restructurings. I fear I've got a lot of long days at the office ahead of me."

"Bummer."

"It means that, on a lot of evenings, I won't be home until pretty late."

"Don't worry, I'm a big boy, I won't get into trouble," and with that Max headed off in search of trousers.

The traffic light ahead turned red. Max's heart skipped a beat. He grabbed the brakes, slowed sharply and twisted his left ankle outward to release the shoe from the pedal.

Nothing.

He twisted again.

Still nothing.

The bike, now stationary, wobbled briefly and then crashed to the ground, Max's feet still firmly attached to the pedals. He squirmed on the asphalt, finally got the shoes released and struggled to his feet. Half-a-dozen drivers looked on in amusement.

It was the second time it had happened that day. The light turned back to green and Max pushed off, repeatedly shoving his foot downward as he tried to reattach the left shoe to the pedal.

Miss.

Miss.

Miss.

At last, the click he had been praying for. He was clipped in. Max traced the route home in his head, trying to figure out whether he could make it back to the house without passing through any more traffic lights.

The pedals were a bitch. Max wondered whether he would ever get used to them. But the bicycle was a thing of beauty. It was a totally different experience from riding his Dad's old aluminum bike. No longer did he feel like he and the bicycle were engaged in a battle of surly recriminations.

The vivid red all-carbon frame absorbed the road's roughness. The gears shifted easily and quietly. The bicycle seemed almost weightless, as though he was magically gliding above the ground. When he drove the pedals, the bike leapt forward like a horse ordered to gallop or a sports car with an edgy accelerator. As he turned the pedals, he endeavored to thrust the shoes not just down but also backward, taking advantage of the clip-in pedals to transfer as much power as possible from his legs to the bike.

"You're too good for me," he whispered. "Way too good. I hope I don't disappoint you."

Max's days were filled with clients to call,

comments from Karen that annoyed, home repairs that needed attending to, drivers who cut him off in traffic and stole his peace of mind. But in the weeks since he had pulled his Dad's old bike from the garage, he had discovered that all that clutter dropped away when he was riding. He would concentrate fiercely on the task at hand—and that had the odd effect of allowing him to think more clearly about the rest of his life. After all the years of meeting his responsibilities to others, Max finally felt like he had time that was truly his own.

As he came to a halt in the driveway, he checked the bike computer: Just over 19 miles at 18.2 mph. Not bad, he thought, as he walked awkwardly into the kitchen, the metal cleats on the bottom of his cycling shoes clattering across the tiled floor. He unzipped his riding jersey and grabbed a banana from the fruit bowl. Tomorrow, should he shoot for more than 20 miles? Would he be able to ride even faster? He downed the banana and chewed it over.

"You missed another client meeting." Alison hit him with the accusation as he walked through the office door. "Remember Mr. Davies, one of your oldest and dearest and most loyal clients?

"Did you cover for me?"

"What do you think? That's the fifth meeting I've handled for you in the past week. There were also the two yesterday and the two while you were spending $65,000 at the bicycle store."

"$6,500," Max corrected her.

"Whatever."

"So how was Mike?"

"Asking about gold."

"Dear God."

"After Monday's dip, it was back up another $30 yesterday. Clients really aren't buying the whole shtick about managing risk, the future is unknowable, nobody has a clue what gold is worth. Like I told you before, we're going to start losing clients."

"They'll be singing our praises when gold implodes. Anything else?"

"Mr. Davies stole the toilet paper from the bathroom."

"Thank you, Lord." Max offered a brief, exaggerated glance at the heavens, his outstretched palms held skyward. "At least our clients haven't totally lost their sense of value."

A lot of toilet paper got stolen. Max wouldn't take a client unless he or she had at least $500,000 to invest. Many had over $1 million. By the standards of their fellow citizens, they were wealthy. But they didn't behave that way. They were frugal to a fault— old cars, modest homes, well-worn clothing. That, of course, was the secret to their financial success. They were incredibly cheap, and hence prodigious savers, and that drove their burgeoning wealth.

As investors, most were mediocre, favoring a hodgepodge of savings accounts and certificates of deposit, with the occasional flyer on some hot stock that would invariably turn cold. Under Max's guidance, they avoided the hot stocks while investing a greater percentage of their money in stocks using diversified index funds. The extra return from investing more in stocks would—assuming the markets were kind—justify Max's fee.

"Are you going to be skipping more meetings?"

Alison asked.

"I don't know. Perhaps. Is that a problem? I think it's good experience for you to meet with clients on your own, without me in the room. If you're going to be a full-fledged financial advisor, it's the next logical step. I want our clients to be comfortable with you. Do you mind talking to them by yourself?"

"Not at all. In fact, I told Mr. Davies that you had asked me to handle his account from now on."

"Did you now?"

"Mr. Davies seemed pleased." As Alison spoke, she tugged at the shoulder of her blouse, pulling up the plunging neckline so it was a little less revealing.

Max could picture the scene, Alison leaning across the conference room table, allowing Mike Davies an unobstructed view. He suspected Mike hadn't minded at all. In fact, Mike probably hadn't heard a single word she had said. At least the old geezer was getting something for his one percent a year.

Max hovered by the counter, waiting for his sandwich. He admired the sundried tomatoes, eyed the fresh mozzarella lounging in a pan of water and looked longingly at the pastries, the fresh cream promising to ooze out upon first bite. But he opted for a simple Italian sub with lettuce and tomato, oil and vinegar, no onions. He loved onions, but clients didn't and he hated the idea of losing a customer because of bad breath.

He scanned the small collection of tables, searching for the woman with the birthmark.

"Looking for somebody?"

The voice startled him. Max turned to his left and

came face-to-face with a pair of surprisingly large blue eyes. Her blond hair was short, almost butch, and her skin was taut.

"I thought I saw my misspent youth," cracked Max, recovering quickly and, with half a smile, inviting her to join the joke.

"Really? And how was it misspent?" The blue eyes were sparkling.

"The usual. Wine, women and song. Mostly wine."

"And then you found God."

"And then I realized I'd become a boring, middle-aged, dead white male."

"You don't look dead."

"It was a close call."

"So you're back wining, womanizing and singing."

"I'm thinking about it."

"I'm Sara. Sara without an 'h'."

"Hello, Sara without an 'h.' I'm Max, also without an 'h'."

Did this woman often strike up conversations with strange men, Max wondered? Did she find him attractive? Had he just won the lottery? Was he starting to perspire? Max forgot all about the woman with the birthmark and snuck a quick look at his left armpit. So far, so good.

"Want to have lunch? I know this great Italian deli." Max could hardly believe it. He sounded witty and charming.

They sat at one of the small round tables, inches apart, their food competing for space with the napkin dispenser, sugar, cream, salt and pepper. A few times, their knees touched and Max felt a surge of electricity course through his body, which is to say, his penis. Like a man woken by the sound of an intruder, he was on sensory overdrive, intensely aware of her, almost breathless.

Max had briefly worried that the lunch might turn awkward because they would run out of conversation. But there was no danger of that: Sara clearly wanted to talk.

She was an only child, a belated arrival that surprised her parents in their 40s, when they assumed all chance of children had passed. By the time she graduated college, they were retired. They pressured her to move back home to Philadelphia. She found herself working as a freelance marketing consultant by day and a nursemaid by night. Her father died in his late 60s. Her mother followed seven years later.

After her mother's death, she married and soon after moved to New Jersey because of her husband's work. Now she was divorced. No, she didn't have any kids. Her marriage had broken up 18 months ago, but the divorce had only just been finalized. No, there hadn't been anybody else.

"I think he had commitment issues," she said. "We dated for years and years but didn't live together, which was fine because I was so busy caring for my parents. In any case, they never liked him, especially my mother. It was easier that we didn't marry."

She continued: "He was always telling me how much he loved me and that, given the situation with my Mom, we could wait to walk down the aisle. But then my mother died and he still didn't want to get married. He said he was happy with the way things were. It was classic behavior, like you read about in the women's magazines. And then, when I threatened to end the relationship, he finally bit the bullet and asked me to marry him. And as soon as we did, everything fell apart. Day after day, he was in a terrible funk. You've never seen a man look so consistently miserable in your life."

She had put him out of his misery—and had been licking her wounds ever since. No, she hadn't dated. Since graduating college, her ex-husband was the only man she had had a serious relationship with and it felt odd to contemplate dating anybody else. No, she really hadn't met anybody she was even interested in. It was tough enough dealing with the divorce and the aftermath. She had felt so rejected, so powerless. She had spent months racking her brain, trying to figure out what had gone wrong, what she could have done differently, what she could have said. She had revisited one conversation after another, parsing his words and trying to uncover the meanings she had missed. She had started running to cope with the stress.

So Max told her about his biking. He recounted his $6,500 shopping trip. She passed no judgment. He told her about his problems clipping into and out of the pedals. She seemed amused. He confided that he thought he could get much better at bicycling. She was encouraging. He was self-deprecating. She was entertained.

Max mentioned Karen in passing, but didn't say he was unhappy. That would blatantly signal his instant infatuation and he didn't want to come across as a sleaze. There would be a time to bare his soul and beg Sara to make it all better. But not yet.

Still, he gave her a business card and procured her email address. He strode purposefully back to the office, a silly smile slathered across his face and a world of possibilities dancing in his head.

*

He stood on the scale in his spandex shorts, the salt from his sweat coating his face. It's hard to look thin in spandex shorts and, truth be told, Max's five foot ten inch frame was far from thin. Nonetheless, the digital scale settled at 169.6. Max couldn't remember the last time he'd been below 170 pounds. Much of the loss would have been the water weight he had shed during the 90-minute ride. Even so, Max declared victory. He had a pleasant sense of physical exhaustion, a sensation he hadn't felt since the sophomore year of high school.

It had been day five of training for the new cross-country season, a blistering hot August day best spent by the pool or at the beach. He was three-and-a-half miles into the team's six-mile training run and the coach was following them on his bicycle, inanely shouting "looking good," "almost there" and "dig deep." Max could imagine nothing sweeter than stopping and letting his howling legs have a few moments of respite. So he stopped, right there in the middle of the workout, and never again started up. The rest of the team disappeared down the street and around the corner, while 16-year-old Max Whitfield began his headlong dash to middle-aged sloth.

Today's ride was mostly flat, but Max liked that. He didn't mind hills. But he loved the feeling of being in a rhythm, driving the pedals for mile after mile, and that came easiest on flat roads with few stop signs or traffic lights. He had averaged 19.1 mph for almost 28 miles. The numbers meant little to most folks and mattered to them even less, but to Max that 19.1 was another milestone on his return to youth.

During the ride, he was stopped at an intersection

by a cop, who signaled he should wait while a group of cyclists went charging by. Max wasn't sure whether it was a true race or just an organized ride. But whatever it was, he had never seen anything like it, the blur of colors, the whirling feet, the riders inches apart. They were there and gone in a flash, and only the policeman's continued presence gave witness to the scene that had just passed. The cop waved Max on.

He probably should have been intimidated. But at that moment, it seemed like a grand theatrical display put on solely for his encouragement. He felt a certain kinship with these other riders. With his costly bicycle and full biking kit, he looked the part. He, too, could be flying down the road in a pack of cyclists suffering from excess testosterone. He could be one of them. After all, he could ride 28 miles at 19.1 mph. Was that fast enough?

Post-shower, he sat in his study, a towel wrapped around his waist, drops of water still clinging to his chest and legs. He listened for Karen's footsteps, but heard nothing as he logged onto his office email. There was another message from Sara. His heart did a quick two-step and he felt an erection press up against the towel.

She told him about her search for a dining-room set for her new townhouse. She mentioned her morning run. She described an email from her ex-husband, talking about his mother's deteriorating health. She wondered whether it was just an excuse to contact her, whether he was trying to revive their relationship.

In his reply, Max recounted his ride, including the racing cyclists he had seen. "Maybe one morning, when I'm biking, I'll see you out running in your short shorts." It was very slightly suggestive. He hit send and wondered how she'd respond.

"How do you know I have short shorts? Have you been in my drawers? LOL."

Puh-leeze, thought Alison, as she cruised through Max's inbox. Poor man gave me his password before going on vacation last summer, but then neglected to change it when he got back.

At first, Alison worried that she had wandered into some ethical gray area. But now, reading Max's emails had become part of her daily routine. It struck her as sound business practice, maybe even necessary self-defense. After all, she was devoting her best years to ensuring Max was successful. It only made sense that she should safeguard her investment, and that meant keeping tabs on everything that affected Whitfield Financial Advisors and her future at the firm.

She had seen the ambition die in her parents and in her friends' parents. She had seen it die in Max. They were all still trying to get ahead, buy the second home, remodel the kitchen, move one step further up the corporate ladder. But their ambition was more circumspect. They were striving for small personal successes. They weren't trying to make a splash in the world.

Alison desperately wanted to make a splash.

"Now, Ali, see if you can try a little harder." It didn't matter whether it was piano, soccer or school grades, her father would offer the same admonishment in the same monotone garnished with the same hint of disappointment. Her mother would stand next to him, silently seconding the sentiment. How many times had that scene been played out? How unworthy of her parents' affection had it made her feel? If they had screamed, the words would have been easy to shrug off. But they were so obviously well-intentioned.

Alison couldn't silence the voice, but she had been surprisingly successful at satisfying it. In her brief career, she hadn't yet failed. The world hadn't yet informed her of her limitations. She hadn't been distracted by a spouse or dragged down by the responsibility of raising a family. Max, she realized, might deserve some credit: He had recognized her talent and gradually given her more responsibility. Her growing sense of success only fed her ambition.

As the office door swung open, she hastily closed out the email program and stood up from her desk, offering a perky smile. "Mr. and Mrs. De Jong, it's great to see you."

As Alison ushered them into the small conference room, she imagined how much grander it would be when she ran the business. The conference room was one of four rooms in the tiny office suite, which also included Max's cluttered office, a bathroom and the reception area, which is where Alison had her desk. It all seemed a little rinky-dink and it made Alison appear to be little more than a glorified secretary.

"I like things the way they are," Max had once told her. "It keeps the overhead low. It isn't like we're growing that fast."

To Alison, it was a sad admission of defeat. When her turn came, she would rent larger offices, hire somebody to oversee marketing, aggressively hunt for new clients, advertise in the local newspaper—and transform Max's $70 million book of business into a $1 billion money-making machine.

"Mr. Whitfield is stepping back from day-to-day management and focusing more on longer-term issues," she began, still half-thinking about how she would lead the business into the big time. "He's asked me to devote more time to meeting with clients."

She pulled out three copies of the portfolio performance report for the De Jong's account, handing one each to the husband and wife and keeping one for herself.

"As you'll see, your account was up 10.2 percent over the 12 months through March 31, which is a good absolute result and above what we project you need to earn to achieve your retirement goals."

"But the S&P 500 was up 15.9 percent," said Mr. De Jong, jabbing his index finger at a number on the report.

"That's true. But the S&P 500 is all stocks and your account is 40 percent in bonds. With your relatively conservative portfolio, you can't expect to keep up with the stock-market averages in a strong market like this. As you know, Mr. Whitfield is very focused on limiting the amount of risk that his clients take."

"But shouldn't we be taking risk in a market like this?" Mr. De Jong persisted. "On CNBC yesterday, I heard gold was up 43 percent over the past year. Why don't we own any gold?"

"As I said, Mr. Whitfield is very focused on limiting risk. He just doesn't like owning something like gold, where it's hard to figure out what it's worth. I can understand your frustration. I don't always agree with Max, either. He can be a little old fashioned. If you're still concerned about your portfolio in three months, feel free to contact me. Maybe the three of us can sit down with Mr. Whitfield and discuss taking the investment strategy in a new direction."

Max sat eighth wheel, more accurately described as dead last. He had never before been on a group ride and he was anxious not to cause an accident that might hurt the other seven and humiliate himself, so he sat at the back of the pack, trying to stay within a few feet of the wheel in front of him. That's what you are meant to do, according to BikeGuy261, who had posted on one of the Internet bicycling forums that Max had taken to reading.

By drafting off the others, Max didn't have to work nearly as hard as the riders who were at the front of the pace line breaking the wind and setting the tempo. The lead rider would change frequently, each taking a brief turn hammering away, while those behind sat comfortably in the draft.

That, at least, was the theory. But even though he was drafting and supposedly getting a chance to take it easy, Max struggled to hold the wheel of the cyclist in front of him as the speed oscillated between 20 and 24 mph. The first 20 miles had been fine. The next ten were bearable. The ten that followed had drained him. Now, they were 42 miles in and the wheels were coming off the bus.

They took a right turn into a slight hill. Max, still nervous about taking corners too tightly, drifted wide and lost the draft. He climbed out of the saddle and stomped the pedals, trying to accelerate. His legs felt like jelly and the bike barely budged. There was no point pretending otherwise. He was cooked.

He sat down, shifted into an easier gear and watched the group disappear into the distance. Tyler, the salesman from the bike shop, and the others had looked dubious when he, the old guy with the paunch, had turned up in the parking lot for the group ride. Sure, he had a fancy bike, pricier than the equipment they rode. But the fancy bike only made him look sillier, Max suspected. Once they realized he had been dropped, they would no doubt joke about him, the old geezer with the money to buy the expensive bicycle but not the talent to go with it.

Maybe they would wait for him at the next traffic light. Max hoped not. He would simply get dropped again and there was only so much humiliation he could take in one day.

"It was 48 miles by the time I got home," he continued. "At the end, I was going maybe 12, 13 mph. I was totally spent. I ate two bananas, climbed into bed and took a two-hour nap."

Max didn't want to be a bore. He knew he ought to let Sara talk and he should play the good listener, just like he had during their first few lunches together. Women liked men who listened attentively. That's what he had been told. But Max couldn't help himself. He had been talking the entire lunch, his sandwich sitting in front of him, barely touched.

"So that's it for the group rides?" asked Sara.

"Are you kidding? This is just round one. Next Saturday, it'll be a different story. I'm going to have pasta the night before, go to bed early, have a big breakfast and put one of those energy drinks in my water bottles. I'm not going to get shown up by a bunch of young punks."

"And what did your wife say?"

Danger, danger. The warning signs were flashing bright red. He should steer clear of this one. "Didn't talk about it—not her thing," Max muttered. He took a deep breath. "So how are you?"

"Ah, it must be time to talk about something other than bicycling."

Max looked crushed. "Sorry. You seemed interested. I guess I was wrong. You know how it is, new hobby and all that."

Sara let him squirm in silence for a few seconds before making amends. "It's great to see you so enthusiastic," she said, reaching over and giving his hand a quick squeeze.

All thoughts of cycling vanished from Max's head and he found himself looking at her with fresh eyes. He could picture her naked, her athletic body, her thin but muscular arms, her small breasts. He gave Sara a goofy grin.

"What?" she demanded.

"Nothing. Just enjoying being here with you. You're beautiful."

She seemed to melt ever so slightly. "I've got to get back to work," she said, taking a final sip of coffee and pushing the remains of her sandwich to one side.

"Me too." In truth, Max felt no need to return to work. Alison could handle things at the office. He wasn't sure there was anything he absolutely had to do that afternoon. But he figured pretending to be a busy professional would make him more desirable. "I think it's time we took our relationship to the next level." He paused for dramatic effect. "How about, next time, we have evening drinks instead of lunch?"

Sara's face lit up. "We could do that."

Karen stood before the director of human resources. "I'm worried we won't make our numbers for the second quarter," she said. "We aren't eliminating employees nearly fast enough. We're meant to hit 2,300 by June 30 and so far we've only had 930 job actions."

The director of human resources didn't look at all concerned. In fact, the words washed over him like a warm shower on a lazy Sunday morning. He was content to lie on the bed and take in her naked body. It wasn't a great body. She had marvelous legs, but her hips were a tad large and her stomach stretched by child birth. But Charles Hastings also knew that he wasn't exactly eye candy. Even though he hadn't yet hit 40, he had long ago abandoned the fight for immortality. He was dumpy, happy and amazed Karen Whitfield had consented to climb between the sheets with him.

"You worry too much," he said, enjoying the handsome curve of her breasts. "Come back to bed."

"This isn't me worrying," she countered, as she gathered up her clothes from the floor. "I like having these goals."

"God, I hate them."

Karen brushed aside the comment. "It's so refreshing after raising two daughters and never knowing whether you're making a difference. Here, we're given a target and we have to meet it. It's cut-and-dried."

"But next quarter, they'll have another target for

us, and another the quarter after that. It doesn't stop. Don't get caught up in all the corporate bullshit. That's why this is fun, here and now, you and me. We're doing it because we want to, not because somebody is telling us we have to get it done by the end of the second quarter. It's almost like we're giving the middle finger to the top brass. How great is that?" Charles's eyes wandered to the ceiling, he exhaled, tried to savor the moment and then returned his attention to Karen. "Did Max seem suspicious when you came home late on Thursday?"

"I fed him the line about going to another all-day employee relations expo in Manhattan. He totally bought it. He's so obsessed with his stupid bike that he doesn't notice anything else."

"That's great. So we can keep seeing each other?"

"Of course, Mr. Hastings."

Gold surged toward $1,700. In San Diego, a retired aerospace engineer admired his fattened portfolio and decided to borrow a little on margin to take his wife to Europe. He didn't particularly like traveling, but his wife had always wanted to see Paris. It would be fun to announce the trip during dinner and watch her bubble over with excitement.

In Greenwich, Conn., a hedge-fund manager saw the trend and figured that, for now, it was his friend. It looked like easy money: Ride the gravy train for a while, make a few bucks and then hop off. It had been a ho-hum quarter so far. Maybe this would goose performance.

In New York, a young advertising account manager sensed Wall Street's blossoming enthusiasm and decided to shift her modest 401(k) into stocks. Her parents had always said they didn't trust the stock market, but that just made it more alluring. She swapped out of bonds and bought the three growth-stock funds with the best one-year performance.

In Atlanta, a couple concluded that maybe their jobs were pretty secure after all and it was time to buy their first home. They had been talking about it for years. They already knew what they wanted: quiet street, three bedrooms, two full baths, kitchen with a breakfast bar, a family room large enough for a big screen TV and a pool table.

And in suburban New Jersey, Alison was fielding calls from clients who were emboldened by the rising stock market and the growing economy, but also anxious that they were missing out on the huge rally in gold.

"Mr. Whitfield, as a matter of policy, doesn't buy gold," she explained for the third time that morning. "He feels there's no way to ascertain what it's really worth. And he says that, if he owned it today, he would be selling, because investors should become less enthused as an investment rises in price."

Max stood by her desk and mouthed the words "thank you." Even after all these years, investors baffled him. They would rush to the department store when there was a sale and prices were lower. But those bargain-hunting instincts deserted them when they managed their investment portfolios. The surest way to get them excited was to jack up the price. In fact, the higher the price got, the more willing they were to buy. It made no sense.

Alison knew Max was right. But she also knew that if Whitfield Financial Advisors didn't give clients at least a little of what they wanted, they would go elsewhere. Their business would certainly suffer. But so, too, would the clients. Before long, they would be lining the pockets of commission-hungry brokers who had no compunction about selling customers what they wanted but shouldn't have.

Already that week, two of Max's 83 clients had walked. Max was quietly pleased, viewing it as confirmation he was doing the right thing. Alison was appalled. She felt her shiny future start to slip away.

"I haven't heard from Mom in ages."

"She's been crazy busy. In the past month, she's twice had to go to Manhattan for these big meetings. She's also been working a lot of late nights. It seems she has to fire a bunch more employees. Some target they have to meet by the end of the second quarter. I'm amazed there's anybody left at that place."

Clare laughed. Conversations with Melanie were often a struggle. But with Clare, he always felt a connection.

"So what have you been up to? With Mom working so much, you must have a ton of time on your hands."

"I wish. Lately, I never feel like I have enough time."

"I know what you mean."

"My dear, sweet daughter, you have no idea," Max chortled. "You have all the time in the world. Or, at least, two or three decades more than me."

"Are we talking about your mortality crisis again?"

"I don't have a mortality crisis. It's not like I wander around terrified I'm going to drop dead at any moment. I'm just very conscious of the ticking clock."

"Sure, Dad, whatever you say."

"Hey, it's something for you to look forward to. You'll be fine through your 20s and 30s, because you'll be so busy pursuing your career, raising kids, buying a home, buying new cars. You'll get caught up in the novelty to it all. But once you get into your 40s, the shit will hit the fan and you'll have a whole new appreciation for what your Dad went through."

Toss in the death of your parents and things get really funky. But Max decided not to mention that cheery thought. Losing his father, just three years after his mother's death, had given him a new perspective. But it wasn't a perspective that left him any mellower. He found himself even more impatient with the nonsense of everyday life.

"So do you wish you were my age again?" asked Clare.

"God, no, I'd never want to be in my 20s again and I certainly wouldn't want to be a teenager. I'm happy being 48. I just want the time back." Max switched gears. "So how are things with you?"

Clare recounted her budding romance with the new boy at work, the kick-boxing classes at the local gym and her delight at the $5 T-shirt she had bought at a flea market. "Remember the presentation I put together, the one the CEO plans to use with the board? He sent me an email saying it looks great."

"I'm so proud of you." He said that often to Clare and Melanie. Max had met too many people— ostensibly mature adults—who remained crippled by their parents' judgment and disapproval. He didn't want to be that parent. For him, Clare and Melanie were the closest he would get to immortality. They would remember him and tell stories about him to their children, and perhaps to their grandchildren as well. He wanted the stories to be good.

"I've been thinking I might try a bike race one of these days," he mused to himself.

"Really?"

"It's just an idea," backtracked Max, as he started to chew over his unexpected declaration. "I was riding a few weeks back and I saw some guys racing. I keep thinking about it. It was just an amazing sight."

"So what race are you going to do?"

"Haven't got there yet. Haven't done anything about it. It's just an idea that popped into my head. But I guess some part of my brain keeps whispering about it."

"That's totally cool."

"Frankly, it scares the shit out of me. But it's funny, that's sort of the appeal. When you're younger, a lot of stuff is scary. But there's less and less as you grow older. Everything gets too damn comfortable. If you don't do things that frighten you, it feels like you're giving up on life."

"But shouldn't life get easier? Isn't that the goal?"

"Yeah, that's the goal," Max conceded. "Or, at least, we tell ourselves that's the goal. It's the carrot we dangle in front of ourselves. But nobody ever gets there and I'm not sure we'd be happy if we did."

"That's really deep, Dad."

"Yeah, I know, I know. That's your old man: He's a really deep thinker."

He thought of little but the asphalt ahead. Look

for potholes. Listen for cars. Watch for manhole covers. Pound the pedals. The world was an episodic blur, anecdotes spied from the side of his helmet, curiosities briefly pondered but which he would never allow himself to stop and investigate.

Max had been cycling for barely two months. He was self-conscious about his ignorance, still not entirely sure what counted as the derailleur, whether he had his seat at the right height and what was the right etiquette when riding in a group. But already he felt like he was no longer the typical amateur. He never just "headed out for a ride." Always there was a plan. Always he was striving to get better. Who was that person he had been 60 days ago? Max had trouble remembering him.

His first outing with the bike shop crowd had been awful. But the following week's ride had been a little less humiliating. He had managed one brief turn at the front of the pace line and he hadn't been dropped until they were almost back at the bike shop. He was easily the oldest and he knew the others were a little scornful. Still, his age was a built-in excuse for falling off the pace and, if he didn't, he triumphed merely by keeping up.

This morning, however, he decided to skip the bike shop's Saturday ride and instead venture out on his own. He liked the solitude and simplicity of riding alone. There was no anxiety about colliding with another cyclist. He couldn't go as fast because there was nobody to draft off. But there was also no waiting around while somebody else fixed a flat. There was no fear of getting dropped by the group. It was just Max, alone with his bike and his thoughts, him against the bike computer.

It was a dance. Push too hard and he would crack. Fail to eat and drink during the ride and he would bonk. Sit up and he would have more power, but he wasn't as aerodynamic as when he grabbed the bottom of the dropdown handlebars and flattened his back. On the computer, below the speed, was his cadence, how quickly he was turning the pedals. If he pedaled too fast in an easy gear, he wouldn't generate much power. If he pedaled slowly in a hard gear, his muscles would quickly tire.

Max used to see the world in terms of towns and neighborhoods. But as he traced his way through the suburban streets, he saw the remains of weathered valleys. He pictured himself clambering up the hill from some long-lost river and skirting across the ridgeline. As the road pitched upward, he climbed out of the saddle and mashed the pedals. "Come on, girl," he whispered to the bike. "We can do this."

Sweat trickled down either cheek, but he felt graceful as he struggled up the hill. He had never thought of himself as an athlete. He had never displayed any particular talent or skill that would catch the eye of others. But now he felt like a performance artist, streaking down the street, offering observers the chance to see what a determined 48-year-old could do. He wondered what Clare and Melanie would think if they saw him. He wondered what Sara would think.

How long would his body hold up? He felt like he had barely used it during the past three decades, so maybe he was good for many more years. But he had also known clients who had started exercising late in life, only to quit soon after because of injuries. He had just rediscovered this part of himself. It pained him to think it might be quickly snatched away.

Ahead, he saw a cyclist. He crouched lower and turned the pedals faster, feeling his competitive instincts fire up and his breathing start to quicken. Sooner than he expected, he was upon the cyclist, only to discover it was an elderly gentleman on a battered bicycle. There were no bragging rights in catching him. Max swooped past in disgust, not even acknowledging the other rider.

He took an extra turn around the neighborhood to get the odometer up to 50 miles and then pulled into the driveway, clipping out on the left and simultaneously punching a button on the computer. The verdict was rendered: 18.9 mph.

"Fuck me," Max exclaimed to nobody but himself. "Pretty fucking impressive for a 50-mile ride. It's a shame I didn't hit 19. Next time. Maybe next time."

He scanned the place for friendly faces and was happy to find none. He had suggested a wine bar that was two towns away but was still nervous they might be spotted.

"Would you like another drink?" The waiter hovered by the table.

"Sure," said Sara, indicating which was her glass. "The sauvignon blanc."

A woman who liked to drink. Max approved. "And I'll have another glass of the shiraz, please." But he ordered it mostly to be social and probably wouldn't drink it. He had to drive both himself and Sara home. He had picked her up at her townhouse, a neighborhood of new construction where the builders had taken pains to mow down every last tree, so there was nothing to hide the shiny vinyl siding. He had murmured nice things about the place. He had lied.

Still smarting from their lunch, Max avoided all mention of bicycling. He talked a little about his daughters and what good kids they were. He told her about Clare's job in Boston. He mentioned that Melanie was going to stay in Chicago for the summer because she had found an internship there. He discussed the travails of his business and the clients he had recently lost. She talked about her latest consulting project and the progress she had made with her home decorating.

It was dull stuff and Max knew it. Things weren't going well. The conversation was limp. She seemed distant. He wasn't sure she had laughed even once. He had anticipated this evening for more than two weeks but, now that it had arrived, it was no match for his imagination. He could feel the moment slipping away. Maybe he would drink that second glass of wine after all.

"Sorry," said Max, who didn't think he had anything to apologize for. But he figured he'd accept blame as a way of acknowledging the lack of spark between them and perhaps getting the evening back on track. "I'm not sure I'm very good company tonight. I must be tired."

Sara scrutinized him. "Are you uncomfortable?"

She obviously doesn't feel sorry, thought Max. He pondered her question. But before he could answer, she hit him with another. "Where's Karen?"

Max was caught off-guard. Sara rarely mentioned Karen's name. It seemed wrong, too familiar, like his two worlds were colliding. "She said she had to work late, that she wouldn't be home until ten."

"She seems to work late a lot. Are you sure she isn't having an affair?"

Max could see weeks of romancing Sara falling apart in a single wretched night. Why was she so pugnacious? "Karen would never have an affair," he said. "It just isn't her. She isn't exactly a passionate person and what little passion she has she pours into her work."

"And what about you?"

Max was caught off-guard again. Boy, this girl really knows how to put a guy on the spot. Things were really turning to shit.

He glanced around the room once again to make sure nobody he knew was there and then brought his gaze back to Sara, finally fixing on her intensely blue eyes. He sensed he had one last shot at salvaging the evening. Max took a deep breath, blew it out slowly and summoned the courage that had often eluded him as a love-struck teenager.

"I'm passionate," he said. "Very passionate. In fact, I'm completely captivated by you."

Sara appeared stunned by his bold declaration and her toughness slipped away. Max seized the silence and reached across the table, touching her cheek and caressing it lightly with his thumb. She closed her eyes and her face took on a dreamy look. Max pulled Sara toward him, taking in her smell and the touch of her lips, acutely aware of that first moment of intimacy.

It was less suffocating this way. Karen straddled Charles, looking skyward, her back slightly arched, her nipples not quite erect, her mind escaping elsewhere.

Charles's house was everything Karen had

expected of a bachelor. No, there weren't television dinners in the freezer and pornography on the coffee table. But it had bland sofas with no pillows, a beautiful cherry sideboard but nothing on it, white walls with precious few pictures. It was a functional house, but hardly felt like a home. It was as clinical as their lovemaking. Karen didn't mind. It suited her mood.

For a quarter century, she had been dutiful. She had thrown herself into motherhood, sacrificing every waking hour to Clare and Melanie. She had driven them to school, to their friends, to youth group, to the young women's self-defense and sexual awareness classes. She had limited frozen foods to three or four nights a week. Always there had been healthy snacks and lightly steamed vegetables. Every morning, she made them nutritious school lunches with juice boxes that contained 100 percent fruit juice. She read them tedious children's books at night. On rainy afternoons, she played those excruciating board games.

Then age 12 became age 13 and suddenly she was no longer their best friend. Sure, she was still needed. But she wasn't wanted. Now that she had fulfilled her biological duty, she was being discarded. Karen was bewildered. How could she so quickly go from indispensible to disposable?

Meanwhile, there was Max. What could she say about Max? She had felt so connected to him early in their relationship, but that had gradually faded. He didn't seem to want or need her. At one time, he had. He had sought her advice. He had relied on her for encouragement. He had depended on her. She truly felt they were partners. Then he, too, became so goddamn independent. Christ, he occasionally emptied the dishwasher and he had even figured out how the washing machine worked.

But it was more than that. His independence was perilously close to selfishness. It was all about him—his stressful days at the office, his problems with clients, his newfound love for bicycling, his desire for a morning quickie after she had already applied mascara. Her daughters had left home, but sometimes it felt like she still lived with a self-absorbed teenager. Now that it was just she and he home alone, their one-sided relationship was no longer obscured by the hurly-burly of family life. Why didn't he ever ask about her day? Why didn't he ever sit down on the sofa and patiently listen to her tale of woe?

She didn't have to work. They could easily live on Max's income. Many of the other neighborhood mothers, even though their children had grown up and left home, either didn't work or worked part-time. They had what Karen derisively dubbed "little jobs." They weren't invested in their work and rarely got stressed by it, and they would happily quit if a parent fell ill or a wedding needed to be planned.

Instead, what they worried about were their adult children. They spent anxious hours comparing notes on their progenies' progress. They tried to recruit Karen into their circle, inviting her to join them for midmorning coffee and to become a member of their book club. But she resisted their entreaties and they quickly stopped asking, preferring not to dwell on this peculiar species of mother.

Karen, for her part, failed to grasp the appeal of carrying the banner of motherhood when there were no longer children around. It simply wasn't enough for her. She didn't want to hang her happiness on her children's success. She didn't want a little job. Instead, she wanted her identity back, separate from her children and separate from Max. It was reminiscent of the months after her daughters were born, especially the second time around, when she was desperate to stop breastfeeding and reclaim her body.

At the office, she was building a new world for herself, one where she once again mattered, where her efforts produced real, measurable results and where her value was reflected in a paycheck that got deposited directly into her bank account every other Friday. She was damn good at what she did, and that realization made her more committed and harder-working.

She hadn't planned on Charles. He would flirt with her, stopping by her cubicle, passing a few words in the office kitchen, chatting with her as they headed back from meetings. She knew he did it with other women. But Karen liked it. It made her feel attractive, in a way she hadn't felt in years, and it didn't hurt that Charles was a decade younger. That made it even more flattering. So Karen reciprocated, playfully touching his arm when making a point and leaning in when they were standing together, so he would notice her scent and feel her warmth.

Why shouldn't she sleep with a colleague? It felt like the final piece of the puzzle, giving her back the emotional excitement she had lost at home. She wasn't sure she loved Charles. In fact, she was pretty confident she didn't. But she loved the courtship and the intrigue. She loved the whispered conversations in the hallway and the knowing smiles, that sense that they had a special world nobody else knew about.

Charles's increasingly heavy breathing brought her back to the moment. "Oh God, oh God, I'm coming," he cried.

That was quick, Karen thought. "That was wonderful," she cooed. Clearly, she would be home earlier than she thought.

He coasted down the driveway in the muted morning light, glancing left to see if any cars were coming, and then took a hard right onto the road. He stood up out of the seat, using his weight to drive down the pedals and quickly get the bike up to cruising speed. As the bicycle computer registered 17, 18 and then 19 mph, he settled into the saddle and tried to bring his breathing under control.

The more Max cycled, the more he understood himself as a cyclist. Certainly, he was no sprinter. He just didn't have the acceleration. He wasn't much good on short, steep hills. He lacked the muscle power to rocket upward. Descents were also a problem. He was carrying less weight than many other riders—he had recently slipped below 160 pounds—and he didn't have the confidence and the bike handling skills needed to hurtle down hills, especially if the hills also had tight turns.

Instead, what he had was the ability to turn the pedals relentlessly and reasonably rapidly for endless miles, which meant he was best suited for flat roads and long climbs. He would make himself suffer and suffer mightily until the ride was done. He was both proud and a little frightened by his ability to eviscerate himself. It was blind perseverance, a mental strength, an unfailing focus.

Except today.

One moment, he would be concentrating fiercely on the road ahead. The next, he could think only of that first kiss. He replayed the scene over and over, savoring it, remembering her lips, her tongue, the smoothness of her skin, the smell of her hair, trying to recall forgotten details.

He thought about the drive back to her townhouse, gripping the steering wheel with one hand and holding her hand with the other, the two of them hiding from the world in the darkness of the car. He recounted to himself the final moments of the evening, sitting in front of her townhouse, embracing across the cup holder, saying goodbye but then turning back for one more kiss.

A few days earlier, he had seen a mother walking down the street holding her three-year-old son's hand. The son was howling, mouth open wide, tears running rivers down either cheek. Max had been struck by the child's uninhibited despair. Could he cry like that anymore, so unrestrained, so publicly? Not a chance. As he had grown older, his range of emotions had seemed to narrow. He was never in the depths of despair, but also never utterly gleeful.

Until now.

He thought he would never again feel this way, that lovesick, overwrought madness of his teenage years, when he would fall passionately in love with a new girl pretty much every two weeks like clockwork. As his marriage to Karen had settled down to humdrum companionship, he thought those feelings had departed forever, that they were something you lose as you grow older, take out a mortgage and start worrying about lawn fertilizer. But they weren't lost.

They were simply buried, shrouded by years of a marriage grown stale, waiting to be rediscovered. Max was again a giddy, crazed teenager.

He had never cheated on Karen—if "cheating" meant having sex with another woman. But even if he hadn't yet crossed that line, he knew that last night he had crossed a line. If Karen found out about yesterday evening, she would probably leave him. Max pondered the possibility and found himself almost relieved.

A sickening pffft interrupted his reverie. "Why?" Max implored the bicycle. "Why does it always have to be the back tire?"

He hauled the bike onto the sidewalk, struggled with the quick release lever and fought the wheel loose of the chain. There was an assumption that, if you were a decent bicyclist, you were also a decent bicycle mechanic. Where was the logic in that? Max cursed his way through the tire change, glad no other cyclists were there to observe his incompetence. He glanced at his watch. Yeah, he would be late again today. Alison was going to be royally pissed.

Gold was stalled at $1,700. In San Diego, a retired aerospace engineer leafed through his Paris guidebook and wondered whether borrowing on margin to pay for a vacation was really prudent. In Greenwich, Conn., a hedge-fund manager looked at his massive, heavily leveraged gold position and toyed with scaling it back. In New York, a young advertising account manager felt a little less ebullient about her three growth-stock funds. In Atlanta, a couple didn't notice much at all. They were too swamped with the paperwork needed for their mortgage application.

And in suburban New Jersey, Alison was debating her next move.

With her last year-end bonus, Max had given her a two percent stake in the firm. It wasn't much. He and Karen still owned the other 98 percent. Still, it was an indication of things to come. She had envisaged Max growing older and gradually turning over responsibility to her. Along the way, she would become a co-partner in the business and eventually take full control, at which point she could put her expansion plans into action. All this would give her time to polish her money-management skills, ingratiate herself with clients and assume some of the gravitas that comes with age.

But she didn't have time. Clients were leaving. Whitfield Financial's assets under management were shrinking. Max might believe the market would soon turn in their favor, but she sure didn't. He should have been working the phones, hunting for new clients to replace those who had left. But instead, he was arriving at the office late, taking long lunches and leaving early. Thanks to bicycling and this woman whose bones he was so desperate to jump, he was totally checked out.

She had recently been handling seven or eight client meetings a week. Max had even asked her to start regularly telephoning their investors to see if they had any concerns. He still made some calls himself, but he seemed increasingly happy to unload the grunt work on her.

"This is another step in your professional development," he had said.

Yeah, right.

What was the man's problem? Didn't he care about the business he'd spent two decades building? It was obvious to anybody paying attention that she was Max's equal as a financial advisor, that she was the one who made the firm tick, that she deserved to be a full partner in the business. Had she wasted six precious years on a company headed for extinction? What would her parents say? Alison winced as if in pain.

She briefly considered setting up her own investment firm and trying to lure clients away from Max. But she was barely 28. No clients in their right mind would trust their life's savings to a 28-year-old. But what if clients weren't in their right mind? What if they were panicked by missing out on the market's gains? What if they had lost their faith in Max? What if they knew what a sleaze he was?

Alison wasn't sure what to do next. But the more she dwelled on the firm's predicament, the grimmer the situation seemed. She had to be prepared. Maybe, if the moment was right and she had the necessary evidence, she would have her chance. She logged onto Max's email account and started printing messages.

He stared at the computer, trying to compose an email to Sara. He had stayed late at the office, after the last client meeting was over and after Alison had departed for the day, so he could write without worrying about anybody bursting in on him.

Here at work, Alison was always walking in and out of his office. At home last Saturday, when he was cruising the Internet, he was startled to find Karen standing behind him, looking over his shoulder. Was she checking up on him? Were they both checking up on him?

He might not be able to spend time with Sara this evening. But at least he could be alone with his thoughts of her. He recalled her smell, her touch, her lips. He imagined making love. What would it be like? He mentally undressed her, painting a picture in his mind of her naked body. With Karen working so many late nights, it would be easy to arrange a rendezvous. Would Sara agree?

He fiddled with the paperweight on his desk and thought about how their relationship would blossom in the coming months. He would leave Karen. Sara and he would buy a home together. Maybe they could get a place further out in the country. He had always wanted to live in the country. How would Clare and Melanie react? He thought they would like Sara. Maybe she would become the caring stepmother they confided in, in a way they didn't confide in their own mother.

What should he write? He gazed absentmindedly at an old picture of Karen and the kids, probably taken seven or eight years earlier. It had sat on the bookcase so long he hardly noticed it anymore.

He focused again on the blank email. He didn't want to sound needy. That would be a turnoff. But he was definitely needy. "Thinking about you," he typed. "When can I see you again?"

Max berated himself. Wrong tone. Keep it light, he reminded himself. Try to be playful.

He started again. "Thinking about your lips," he wrote. "We should get together again." That was cute, Max thought.

"I'd also like to see the rest of you," he added. That was cute—and flirtatious. He added the obligatory smiley face. Or was the smiley face too girly? Probably. Even so, he decided to go for the smiley face.

His fingers hovered above the keyboard, debating one another, before tapping out a final sentence: "Maybe we could spend the afternoon together—and the evening, too."

Then he hit the send button. How would she respond? How often did she check her email? It always seemed to take her ages to reply.

Clare sat in her modest Cambridge apartment, laptop in front of her. In truth, it wasn't an apartment, just a bedroom and living room. There was also a bathroom down the hall that only she was meant to use, though that was a promise the owners regularly broke.

They were a couple in their late 50s—just a decade older than her parents—who had started renting out the rooms after their own children had left home. Clare felt a little self-conscious creeping in late at night, especially if she'd had a few drinks. It was like she was back home again, living with her own parents.

Still, for Clare, struggling to get by on slightly less $40,000 a year in one of the country's most expensive cities, the price had been right. It meant she didn't need to split costs with a roommate. Sharing? After four years of college and a year-and-a-half in the work force, she was so done with the roommate thing.

She compared the two emails from her parents.

Both were upbeat. Her mother was raving about work. Her father was raving about his latest ride. But neither email mentioned the other parent.

Was it always that way? Did they always lead such separate lives? She tried to recall.

Clare remembered them as a tag team. Her mother would drive them to school events. Her father would pick them up. They might have been apart. But they were a team, picking up the slack so the other could have a few quiet moments.

But now that she and Melanie were no longer around, they seemed to have lost their rationale for teaming up. Clare didn't recall her parents having a bad relationship. But she couldn't honestly say what sort of relationship they had. More than anything, they struck Clare as an efficient child-rearing operation, skilled at moving their two daughters through the day and getting the necessary tasks done.

Was that the way it was? Do parents become so focused on raising their children that they lose their identity as a couple and lose sight of what had brought them together, so there's nothing to bind them once the kids depart? Just when they could again spend endless hours with one another, do they discover they no longer want to?

Clare vowed she would never allow that to happen to her and her future husband, whoever he might be. But she also suspected that many such vows had been made and subsequently made to look foolish.

It was one of the longest days of the year, so it would have been a great morning to ride. He could have headed out early, before the New Jersey heat and humidity settled in, notched a quick 15 miles and still got to the office in plenty of time. But this morning, Max didn't ride. He didn't want to be tired and he didn't want to feel rushed.

He took his time with the razor, trying to shave as closely as possible. He was worried about scratching Sara and he knew Alison would be suspicious if he headed to the bathroom to shave in the middle of the day. He put on deodorant, but tried not to put on too much. He skipped the aftershave. He had bottles of the stuff, given to him by Karen and Melanie and Clare and Alison for father's day, Christmas, birthday, Valentine's Day, Arbor Day, you name it. Women love to buy aftershave—and men hate to wear it. Would women ever notice? Or did they just presume that they had bought the wrong aftershave and that all would be perfect once they figured out the right brand?

He examined himself in the mirror. He figured he was acceptable enough. All the exercise had taken some weight off. But his upper body wasn't exactly toned. His biceps looked a little puny. His chest was small and pasty. Only his forearms were tanned, because they were the only part of his upper body left exposed by his riding shirts. His stomach wasn't exactly defined. But his legs looked good. Would Sara notice his legs? Men regularly checked out women's legs, but he wasn't sure such admiration was ever reciprocated.

What about his penis? Would that pass muster? Max suspected it was pretty average as penises go, not that he had made an extensive study of the subject. He had never had any complaints but, then again, there hadn't been that many women in his life to complain. After all, he had spent the last 25 years sleeping with the same woman, and there hadn't been many others before Karen. Would Sara enjoy his lovemaking? He thought of himself as a gentle, thoughtful lover, but based on what, he wasn't sure. The truth was, lovemaking with Karen was serviceable at best.

He picked out his favorite shirt, one that outlined his torso without being too tight. He found the tie he always wore with it and, from the closet, fished out the trousers he had just bought, with a smaller waist that matched his shrinking stomach.

He had got his hair cut a few days earlier, so it had time to grow in a little and didn't look too groomed. His flecks of gray hair seemed more prominent when his hair was recently cut, but he figured that made him look distinguished. He brushed and combed it into place, and then gave himself one last look over.

"Ready or not, here I come," he muttered to the mirror.

They had both blocked their calendars for a two-hour stretch at lunchtime. They left the corporate campus separately, each taking their own car and meeting outside Charles's house.

For weeks, Karen has been on tenterhooks, anxious that her late nights might give her away. To be sure, she had been careful. She showered whenever she left Charles, so the smell of their lovemaking wouldn't be on her. In fact, she worried that she might smell too clean after what was supposedly a 14-hour workday. She told Max elaborate lies, filled with details about imaginary meetings she had to attend and imaginary workers she had to fire. She worried that maybe she was being too clever and that one day she would be tripped up by some long-forgotten lie. She even created an entire scene that involved calling security to have a belligerent employee escorted from the office.

And Max bought it, hook, line and sinker. He seemed totally clueless.

Despite her frequent absences, Max also seemed increasingly cheerful. Could it really be the bicycling? Did he spend his days in a happy haze, constantly high on endorphins? Karen found it baffling. He had gone from aging slob to budding athlete in just a few short months. He was also spending more time on the computer. Max said he was trying to learn more about cycling. Maybe he was looking at pornography. She once had to fire an employee for watching porn on his office computer.

Max had started heading into the office later. Karen had often suggested that he take it easier, that he didn't have to work so hard now that his business was well-established. Was he finally taking her advice?

He never objected when she said she'd be home late. Indeed, he asked remarkably few questions. He would just listen to her carefully fabricated excuses and then drift off. He had even gone out the other night when she was supposedly working late. She'd got home just after 9 p.m., not ten like she had said, and Max arrived home shortly afterwards, looking a little flustered at finding her there. He said he didn't feel up to cooking anything, so he had grabbed a drink and some hors d'oeuvres at a nearby wine bar. That was odd. Max hated eating alone in restaurants. Was this part of his ongoing self-reinvention? What was happening with Max?

He also wasn't asking for sex as often as he used to. At first, Karen was relieved. The frequent sessions with Charles were more than enough. But now it was starting to seem a little odd. Despite his selfishness, no matter how clueless he seemed, she felt that Max at some level depended on her. Did he subconsciously sense that she was cheating and that was why he was avoiding her? How devastated would he be if he learned of her office romance?

"I'm a little concerned about Max."

"You think he's suspicious."

"Not at all. That's the thing. He seems totally lost, like he doesn't care about anything but his bicycling."

"Well, that's wonderful," said Charles, quickly realizing that maybe that wasn't the right reaction. "I mean, I'm sorry he seems lost. Maybe something's going on in his life that you don't know about. Who knows, maybe he's having an affair."

"Don't be ridiculous," retorted Karen, waving her hands dismissively. But the idea stuck. Could Max be having an affair? It seemed implausible. But despite a ferocious effort, she couldn't rule it out.

"So what's your fancy?" she asked as they turned away from the reception desk and headed toward the elevators. Max had assumed they would meet at her townhouse. Sara had insisted on a hotel. They couldn't stay all night, but he had cleared the entire rest of the day: He had said to Alison he was taking the afternoon off and told Karen he had dinner with a client.

He paused before replying. "We could get a

drink," he offered. "I've heard they have a pretty good bar here. I guess I also wouldn't mind having a quick shower," he added, figuring it might be wise to wash away a little of his nervous perspiration.

He saw a twinkle in her eye.

"You could join me."

The smile widened. As the elevator doors closed, Max reached up, ran his fingers through her hair and pulled her lips toward his. He kissed her gently, barely touching her mouth, and heard her sigh.

When they reached the sixth floor, he took her hand and led her to the room. He fumbled with the key card, gave her a crooked smile and finally the door was shut behind them. They kissed again, harder this time, their eyes closed.

"I'd still like to have that shower."

She laughed. "Me too."

He flipped off his shoes, she followed suit and they met again in the middle of the room. He kissed her neck and let his hand glide down her body, stopping at her thigh and then heading back up. As he lightly touched her breasts through her blouse, he felt her shudder.

Max had imagined this moment, undressing her slowly and wondering what she would think as he removed his clothes. Would she see an out-of-shape 48-year-old or the newly athletic Max?

But nothing happened slowly. Suddenly, her jacket was on the floor and her fingers were unbuttoning his shirt. They backed their way toward the shower, shedding clothing as they went.

With the water raining down on them, he played with her nipples with his tongue and slid his hand between her legs, discovering her clitoris and slipping a finger inside her vagina. Her breathing deepened and he felt her heart beat faster.

"Let's get into bed."

They dripped their way across the bathroom floor and into the bedroom. She lay on the bed, the water glistening on her skin, and he sat beside her, exploring her with a light touch, drinking her in.

He marveled at her body. He couldn't help but compare her to Karen: She was so much leaner, her breasts so much firmer, she seemed to have a far younger woman's body. Sara caught him staring. She looked embarrassed. "You're more beautiful than I imagined," he whispered, which prompted her to blush even more deeply.

He kissed one breast and cupped the other, then let his lips caress her stomach as they headed toward her vagina. He teased her clitoris with his tongue and felt her body come alive. She ran her fingers along his penis and held his testicles.

It had been a while. Maybe he should have masturbated the day before or at least the day before that. That way, he wouldn't be quite so primed to come. But there was no doubt: He was primed now. He tried to disengage his own feelings and focus on her, focus on her quickening breath, even as he tried to slow his own.

She moaned.

He climbed on top, stroking the inside of her thighs and spreading her legs. She guided his penis inside. He was enveloped in the warm wetness, the firmness of her vagina, that sense of arriving at a place you never want to leave. When had he last been here? When had it last felt like this?

He rested on one arm and touched her with the

other hand, watching that distant gaze come into her eyes. He thrust gently back and forth and then harder still, as he realized he had taken charge of his feelings and it wouldn't all end too quickly. It was always so fast with Karen. Why was it different now? He wondered whether, with Karen, all that mattered was his orgasm, whereas making love with Sara was about so much more.

They paused, lying there quietly for a while, kissing and smiling, locked together, delaying the climax, not wanting it to end. But slowly, inevitably, they started to move. He reached down, found her clitoris and gently touched her. She moaned again.

He could feel her start to come, like a train in the distance, the sound barely audible at first but growing closer all the time. He teased her a little, touching her and then stopping, but that only excited her more. He sensed the anticipation in her body.

"I'm coming," she called out. "Oh God, I'm coming." Max couldn't take his eyes off her. He watched her climax, her eyes shut, her face turned partially away, her lips slightly pursed. He leant over, quietly kissed her lips and began to move again.

"I think it's your turn," she said, her eyes laughing.

Max was more than ready. He relaxed a little, stopped holding back and it all came lightning fast. He felt the orgasm begin at the base of his penis, the momentum building, getting closer, closer still and then came the surge, a momentary pause and the almighty explosion. Every thrust brought further, smaller explosions, one after another, until the tip of his penis became too sensitive and he stopped, huddled over her, breathing hard. "God, that was great. God, it's been way too long."

They lay on the bed, looking at each other, their legs interlocked. He breathed in her smell and the crooked smile returned. "I'm not sure I should say this, but I love you."

Sara turned serious and then her face softened. "That's very sweet, Max. Maybe we should get that drink."

SUMMER

He had been awake a mere 35 minutes when he hit the road. It was just enough time to down a cup of coffee, brush his teeth, shave, pull on his cycling gear and retrieve the bike from the garage.

Usually, he was sluggish at first, his body still weary from the day before. But today, even though his legs had the shortest of time to come alive, he was hammering it from the get-go, ripping down the streets as he tried to wrestle his swirling emotions into some sort of coherence.

It was like his personality was split. Part of him was furiously pounding the pedals. His eyes darted between the road ahead and the tiny computer screen on his handlebars, trying to keep his pedaling speed at right around 95 revolutions per minute. He monitored his heart rate, dancing on the edge of breathlessness. He tried to keep his arms and hands relaxed, saving the tension and the focus for his spinning legs.

But the other part of him was consumed by Sara, by memories of her body and of the night before. He thought of her breasts, the taste of her vagina, how it felt to be inside her. He had expected to feel guilt but he had none. Was he so amoral? Was this an indication of how little he cared for Karen?

When he walked into the house shortly after 10 p.m., he couldn't believe how blasé he was. He told Karen about his client dinner with an easy confidence, even as she peppered him with questions. "I must be a born liar," he boasted to himself. He was rapidly approaching 50 and yet it was as if he were discovering who he was for the first time. He was an athlete, a charmer, a lover, a rake. Thirty years after he graduated from high school, he had finally become the cool kid in class. Who'd have thought?

Max consoled himself with the conviction that, even if he wasn't honest with Karen, he was at least honest with himself. He saw his affair, as well as the bicycling, for what they were: An aging sort-of-successful financial advisor making a last stab at recovering the passion and vitality of youth. He was 48 and counting, and the clock ticked loudly in his head. His fight against time was a messy, self-indulgent business, but he didn't care. He'd rather go out kicking and screaming. He felt alive. It was better than the alternative.

He tried to think objectively about who Sara was and why he found her attractive. But he couldn't get beyond the fact of his attraction. He loved, more than anything, the feeling of being in love. It transported him back three decades, to age 18, when wondrous things seemed ahead of him and time was still in his favor.

Max had assumed that age marched with a white flag, surrendering passion as the years slipped away. Sara had blown that apart. His giddy infatuation was unseemly, maybe even silly, like the serial infatuations of his teenage years. Was this what adult life was all about? Was it about trying to recapture magical moments from our youth—or, at least, moments we now recall as magical? Did that also explain the biking?

He was aware of a crucial disparity between his and Sara's situations. She was alone; he already had someone. She would want him to leave Karen. This was more than a fling for her. She was looking for a new partner.

The sweat built up under his helmet and escaped down his cheeks, stinging his eyes and obscuring his sunglasses. Max relished the harshness of the ride. His loveless relationship with Karen had gone on long enough. He should be with Sara. That, he knew, was what he wanted. He lowered his head and drove for home.

As Max straddled the bike in the driveway, his chest still heaving, he checked the computer: 13.6 miles at 20.2 mph. He had never before come close to riding so fast on one of these short early morning outings, when his body was barely awake. Max took it as a sign from the cycling gods.

They approved.

The good news was, Whitfield Financial Advisors still had $67 million under management at the end of the second quarter, only $3 million less than three months earlier. The bad news was, the number of clients was down from 83 to 73. Despite an average gain of eight percent over the past three months, clients were heading for the door.

"At times like this, you discover that some clients aren't right for your practice," pronounced Max, sounding like a Sunday school teacher delivering a profound life lesson. "It's okay that they leave. If they don't buy into the firm's philosophy, they're going to be high maintenance and we don't need the hassle."

Alison listened to the lecture in silence, fighting her sense of panic. The business was falling apart, and Max seemed content to sit back and let it happen. Why wasn't he pounding the pavement, trying to find new clients? Would Whitfield Financial Advisors go out of business? Would he have to lay her off?

Despite his outward bravado, Max wasn't feeling so good himself. He had lost clients before. But over the past three months, he hadn't managed to attract a single new investor to replace the departures. Admittedly, he hadn't been devoting much time to hunting for new clients. He never enjoyed playing salesman and had hoped those days were behind him. In recent years, most of his new investors had come from referrals from existing clients. But existing clients weren't referring friends. His reputation wasn't attracting potential customers. He was clearly wildly out of touch with today's heady market.

From an investment perspective, that didn't bother him. Popularity was the market's flashing red warning sign. If an investment was attracting a crowd, it was almost certainly overpriced. Lots of folks had bought, pushing up the price. Eventually, the buyers would have done all their buying and there would be nowhere for the price to go but down.

But whatever happened in the market, Max figured his business was in for a rough time. If gold kept rising, he would lose more clients. What if gold declined? The panic would likely also drag stocks lower. Even Max's clients, with their conservative portfolios, could easily suffer losses of seven or eight percent.

Assuming he didn't lose any more clients, that might leave Max with $62 million to manage, which would give him $620,000 in revenue based on his one percent fee. His costs were pretty much fixed at $350,000, so the lost revenue would come straight out of his income. It would hurt a little. But he would probably still be taking home $270,000 a year. With that sort of income, he could continue to live comfortably and save a decent amount each month.

But all this assumed he could hang on to his remaining clients. That looked like an increasingly shaky assumption. A few clients had mentioned being called by other advisors, who seemed more than happy to offer riskier portfolios heavily laden with gold.

Max was stuck—and it didn't seem like there was a whole lot he could do. If he caved in and bought gold, he might make some clients happy. But he would alarm others, who would be unnerved by his sudden sacrificing of principle. He gnawed on his pen and wearily contemplated the disgruntled clients who would call in the days ahead.

He thought he saw a few eyes roll as he coasted into the parking lot. It had been weeks since Max had last joined the bike shop's Saturday morning ride. He knew what the dozen other cyclists were thinking: Hey, look, the old dude is back. I wonder how long it will take before we drop him this time.

Max was determined not to be dropped. After a week of ever-so-patiently answering the objections of ornery clients, he was ready to unleash his frustrations on the road.

"Okay, let's roll." It was Tyler, the store's salesman and ride leader. "Take it easy down to River Road and then we'll crank it up."

They started up at a casual 16 mph. The other cyclists chatted with each other, bantering about how little they had ridden over the past week. Max knew it was all lies. These guys lived to strut their stuff on Saturday mornings. They'd been training hard all week so they could shine today. He hung at the back of the pack, feeling like the odd man out.

As they turned onto River Road, one of the cyclists went to the front and began wailing away at 23 to 24 mph. The others scrambled to form a pace line behind him. Everybody was itching to get to the front, take a long pull and prove their worth.

Not Max. He snagged a spot at the back of the pace line. As cyclists rotated off the front, he eventually found himself leading. He kept it at 23 mph, counted to 60 and pulled off. He figured 60 was respectable, enough to show he was pulling his weight in the pace line without blowing himself up.

He drifted to the back of the line and tucked behind the last bicyclist. As soon as he was safely in the draft, he grabbed one of his bottles of Gatorade and took a long swig. Tyler had said the route was 50 miles. Anything above 40 and Max knew there was a serious chance of bonking. He needed to consume calories early and often.

Ten miles in, he began to relax. His legs were feeling good and he knew he could handle the pace. He hadn't ridden the day before, figuring it would give him fresher legs for the group ride. Most of the others rode every day. But they were younger. Max tried to take off at least one and sometimes two days each week.

As the miles piled up, the testosterone started to fade. The speed dropped to 22 mph, sometimes 21. Some of the guys were taking shorter pulls at the front. Max stuck to his 60 count.

There was an anonymity to these group rides. You spent two or three hours staring at the backside of other cyclists, sitting in their slipstream, occasionally catching the smell of their sweat, maybe taking a little mucus splattering from their snot rockets, and yet you might not know their names, let alone anything about their lives. White or blue collar? Gay or straight? Married or divorced? Max had hardly a clue.

Instead, he knew these riders by the make of their bikes and the logos on their jerseys. And, of course, by their ability. Some were climbers, some were sprinters, some were big engines who liked to sit at the front of the pace line and drag it for miles. Everybody knew who was strong and who was likely to disappear off the back of the pack.

But being strong wasn't enough. You also needed a little cunning. The strong rider who took long pulls at the start of the ride might be suffering mightily at the end, while the weak cyclist who hid out in the pace line could finish surprisingly strong. Max couldn't outride most of these guys, but maybe he could be smarter.

He looked at his odometer: 42 miles. Too soon. He rotated through the pace line a few more times, then checked again: 45 miles. Better. When he hit the front, he hunched over the handle bars, flattened his back and slowly cranked up the speed, 21 mph, 22, 23, 24. He relaxed his face and tried to keep his breathing under control, even as his legs started to burn.

After three minutes, he pulled off and surveyed the damage. The pace line was down to nine. Three riders had been dropped. He tucked in at the back and checked the speed. The group was still moving at close to 24 mph. Max may have started the hammerfest, but the others weren't about to get shown up. The self-destructive surge to the finish was underway.

Max felt the speed slow and took his eyes off the wheel in front. The pace line had broken in the middle. Somebody else had blown up. Max jerked his bike left, sprinted past flagging riders and caught the back of the truncated pace line. There were only five cyclists left, Max included. If anything, the pace picked up a little, the speedometer occasionally hitting 25 mph. Max could feel the effort start to bite.

There were just two miles left. When his turn came, he took a quick pull at the front and then dropped to the back of the pace line. His heroics were over for the day. They turned onto the street leading to the bike store. The other cyclists jockeyed for position as they wound up for the final sprint. One rider jumped and the others immediately counterattacked. Max let them go. His legs were cooked and, in any case, he knew he was no sprinter.

He rolled into the parking lot a dozen seconds

after the rest. If they were aware that he'd bailed on the final sprint, they didn't show it.

"Nice ride, man," said one of the kids, giving Max a fist pump that he awkwardly reciprocated. "Nice pull at the end there. You were really flying."

He hung up the phone with Al Hamilton, exasperated. He had tried the "nobody knows what gold is really worth" argument. That didn't work.

So he went for the "there's a seller for every buyer" argument. "When you buy an investment, you never know who's on the other side of the trade," Max explained. "Yes, the seller might be the guy who lives next door. But it's more likely to be a professional money manager with decades of experience and access to the latest market research. As a buyer, you've got to ask yourself, 'Am I confident I know more than the seller?'"

When that failed, Max talked about the reasons for managing money, how it wasn't about beating the market or earning the highest possible return. It was about amassing enough dollars to pay for important goals, like retirement or a child's college education. "You shouldn't put those goals at risk by being unnecessarily aggressive," he argued.

"Sorry, Max," said Mr. Hamilton, cutting him off and sounding impatient. "I've made my decision. I know you've done well for me over the years. But the markets have changed and I'm not sure you're the right person to handle my money anymore." And with that, Whitfield Financial Advisors was down to 72 clients.

"We lost another," Max told Alison. "Mr.

Hamilton. He's probably been a client for 15 years." This time, Max didn't bother putting on a brave face. Maybe Alison was right. Maybe he had been too stubborn. Maybe he should have pandered to clients a little more.

"Max, could we sit down later today and talk about the future of the business?" Alison's voice had a toughness Max couldn't recall hearing before. "I'd like to know how you see my role evolving and how things might change as you approach retirement."

Max, still mentally replaying the conversation with Al Hamilton, gave Alison a weary, distracted nod. Retirement? What was she talking about? "We can do that at some point," he said. "Maybe in a few weeks, when things quiet down. I need to clear my head. I'll be back in an hour or so."

All week, he had been looking forward to today's lunch. But now that the moment had arrived, his mind was elsewhere. He tried to shove aside the Hamilton conversation and whatever it was Alison had been asking about.

It had been 13 days since he had seen Sara, since their long afternoon and evening of lovemaking. He had wanted to see her the very next day. But Sara put him off, saying she had a big project to wrap up for a difficult client. Max thought about pressing the point—after all, couldn't she spare an hour for lunch?—but he didn't want to be pushy.

The intervening 13 days had given him plenty of time to think. He found himself anxious about the relationship one moment, confident they had something truly special the next. He spent hours daydreaming about the life they would have together, the restaurants they might go to, the vacations they might take, the old farmhouse they might buy. Max knew he was jumping the gun and yet he couldn't wait to talk to Sara about such plans.

"Hey, how are you, stranger?"

Sara responded with a broad grin. "It's great to see you."

"Ditto. It's been a hell of a week. What about you? Finish your big project?"

"Sure did."

"So you think you might be able to play hooky again some afternoon?"

"It depends who's asking," she said, pretending to be coy.

"It's this wild-and-crazy guy, hotshot money manager, super-fast bicyclist, super-gentle lover."

"Mr. Max Whitfield, I think you're obsessed."

"With cycling?"

"With everything."

"I'll confess to being obsessed with you."

Sara frowned. "I'm not sure I want that."

"Really?" said Max, thrown on the defensive. "That doesn't sound good. I just love spending time with you."

"I know you do," said Sara, giving his arm a playful squeeze. "And I love being with you. But…." Her voice trailed off.

"But what?"

"I know you're unhappy with your wife. But we've only just met each other."

"Am I coming across too strong?"

"Maybe a little." She gave Max a look that softened the words. "I'm really fond of you, Max Whitfield. I really think you're special. But remember, you're the first person I've been involved with since my divorce. I'm still getting used to this. I've read a lot of articles about relationships. It's a big mistake, if you're getting involved with somebody after a bad breakup, to let the relationship get too heavy too quickly."

Max gave her a somber look. But he felt elated. Sara was clearly frightened by the depths of her feelings for him.

"Don't worry, I hear you," he said, deciding he would save mention of the old farmhouse for another day. "We'll take it slowly."

Each evening's broadcast lasted for hours and the decisive battle might not come until the final few minutes of the stage. Even so, Max couldn't take his eyes off the screen.

Before this year, he had been only vaguely aware of the Tour de France. Now, he was consumed by each day of the three-week race. He was captivated by the tactics, the riders, the jerseys, the French countryside, the publicity caravan, the screaming fans crowded either side of the mountain roads. He winced when the riders crashed, agonized as they struggled up climbs so steep they were "beyond classification" and crept closer to the television as the riders prepared for the final sprint. It was a grueling, beautiful sports spectacle with an entire country as the stadium.

Max grabbed the phone. "Clare?"

"What's up, Dad?"

"Just sitting here watching the Tour de France."

"Where's Mom?"

"Where do you think? She working's late again."

"You sound pissed."

"Not at all. It's fine. Honest. Your mother wouldn't want to spend the evening watching bicycling on TV. I find it relaxing, especially after all the stuff that's going on at work."

"Are things okay with the business?"

"Not great. We've been losing clients because of the market."

"That's happened before, right?"

"It's never been as bad as this."

"You must be going nuts trying to find new clients to replace the ones you've lost."

"Actually, I haven't done much of that. Truth be told, I can't muster a lot of enthusiasm for work these days. It just feels like such a grind. But at least I get to come home and watch the Tour. It's unbelievable. These guys are total animals."

"Do you imagine yourself there, riding the Tour?"

"Sure, it's the usual middle-aged fantasy, thinking you'll discover you have some great untapped athletic talent, give up your day job, train like crazy and end up beating the best in the world. But it isn't going to happen. I'm struggling to ride 130 miles a week. These guys do that in a single day."

"Yeah, but what if you'd started riding when you were younger?"

"Do I sit here and think, 'I coulda been a contender'? I may be delusional, but I'm not that delusional. The pros are incredible athletes. It's like they're from another planet. Still, it's fun to watch, because I have some sense for the pain and the effort involved. It's fun to think about riding in the peloton, flying through these tiny French villages and pounding my way up these huge mountains. You should try watching some evening."

"I really don't have time."

"It might inspire you to start riding. Then we could ride together whenever you're home."

"Dad, you're obsessed."

Obsessed? There was that word again. "I guess I can't help myself. After all these years of doing the same thing week after week, it's like this whole new dimension has been added to my life. All of a sudden, at least part of my day seems exciting again, like it was when I was your age."

"Trust me, my life isn't all excitement. Right now, the most exciting thing I want to do is climb into bed and fall asleep. Today totally kicked my butt."

"Sounds like you've also got trouble at the office."

"Not trouble. Just a lot of work and not enough hours in the day. I sure don't have time to go bicycling all over the countryside like you. So does watching the Tour de France make you want to do a race? Are you still thinking about it?"

"Christ, I'm starting to wish I'd never mentioned the idea. Yeah, I'm thinking about it, still thinking about it. But that's as far as I've got."

"Mr. Hastings, it's good to see you."

"It's good to see you, Mrs. Whitfield."

Charles and Karen took a table in a corner of the company cafeteria and glanced around, making sure nobody was close enough to hear their conversation. They both delighted in the furtiveness of their meeting, hiding in plain sight, pretending to have a business lunch while really having a meeting of lovers. Forget attraction, physical or otherwise. Their shared secret was aphrodisiac enough.

"I've been thinking about what you said, about Max having an affair."

"It was just a thought," mumbled Charles, who didn't want Karen spending too much time pondering the morality of extra-marital affairs. "I could be completely wrong."

"His behavior has been a little odd, dinners with clients, dinners out on his own, spending hours on the computer. But when I quiz him, he's always got a good excuse."

"So maybe there's nothing going on."

"Maybe. But the idea really bothers me. I know it doesn't make any sense given...." Karen left the sentence unfinished, preferring not to describe her relationship with Charles. Was it an office romance? A fling? Occasional mediocre sex? "But after all I've done for him and Clare and Melanie, it would be a real slap in the face if he was screwing around. I deserve better."

You're right, thought Charles, you aren't making any sense. But he figured that probably wasn't the most diplomatic response. "I've got some good news," he said, hoping to change the subject. "I put in the request."

"You did?" Karen was beaming, all concerns about Max's fidelity forgotten.

"It could take a few months," Charles cautioned. "The chief operating officer has to sign off on it and he's always slow to sign, especially if it means a pay raise for somebody. Remember, we're supposed to have a salary freeze right now. He'll blather on about resource allocation and diversity underpinning a strong corporate culture and sending the right signal.

And just when we're both ready to blow our brains out, he'll sign. All being well, within a few months, you'll be the deputy head of human resources."

Karen ignored Charles's cynicism. She wasn't cynical. She hungered for the promotion, but not for the power or the money. She just wanted the acknowledgment, the tangible proof that she was truly good at what she did. She wanted confirmation that she had chosen well, that she was right to turn her back on the aging minivan mommies who gathered childless in the coffee shop to swap stories of their adult offspring's successes.

Karen couldn't believe it had been so easy. She hadn't had to badger Charles or get all pouty. She hadn't had to suggest sex might be a little less forthcoming. She simply mentioned the idea. He had given her a long look, as if sizing her up, before announcing, "That could be arranged."

"Are you sure it was a good idea to put in for the pay raise as well as the promotion?" asked Karen. "What if they find out about us?"

"Don't sweat it. This sort of thing goes on all the time. Nobody will care. "

"It makes me nervous."

"Don't be. It'll be fine. You just need to be a little patient. Like I said, it could take a few months to get approved."

"Ah, the things we'll do together," said Karen.

"Yes, the divisions we'll eliminate, the people we'll fire."

They both laughed just a little too loudly, eliciting looks from nearby tables. They shushed each other, then started laughing again, but more quietly this time.

*

Max thought of his day as a series of small pleasures. It started with morning coffee and continued with the newspaper. Then, there was breakfast and another cup of coffee sitting at his desk in the office, lunch, a glass of wine when he got home in the evening and, finally, dinner. With the exception of the newspaper, all involved consuming food or drink. Clearly, his ideas of pleasure hadn't progressed much beyond that of his hunter-gatherer ancestors.

Now, he had two other daily pleasures to add to his list: his morning ride and the emails from Sara. The ride was the duty before the reward, though most days it hardly seemed like duty. Still, he knew that, if he rode five or six days a week, there was no real limit to how much he could eat.

In fact, despite the joy he took in eating, he sometimes struggled to consume enough. He had taken to tracking his weekly cycling mileage, pushing the total from 130 to 140 and now 150. He would endeavor to clock 100 miles during the course of his Saturday and Sunday rides, and then squeeze in another 50 during the week. He was in the greatest shape of his life and yet he looked scrawny and maybe even a little emaciated. As his face grew more gaunt and his belly disappeared, clients would ask if he had been sick. Alison had made a few scathing remarks. Even Karen commented. Max detected a touch of concern in her voice.

But Sara didn't seem to mind. She had a similar build thanks to the running, with thin but muscular legs and a small but firm chest. In fact, they looked similar enough that he sometimes wondered whether they might be mistaken for brother and sister, rather than lovers.

He eagerly awaited her emails, checking his inbox constantly. She wrote with fair frequency, but he got the sense she was in no hurry to respond. Sometimes, he would hear back within a few minutes, but occasionally it took a full 24 hours. He knew she spent the entire day parked in front of the computer. It nagged at him.

Max contemplated asking Sara about it. Early on, it seemed like they could say anything to one another. But that window had closed. Now, he didn't want to roil the waters. Was their relationship that tenuous? Was he that afraid of her answer?

"Got the champagne, like you asked," he wrote. Max didn't really care for all the bubbles and he thought the stuff overpriced, but who cared? "See you at the hotel at 1 p.m. Can't wait."

He glanced at his watch. He knew he had plenty of time, but he was still antsy to leave. To kill a few minutes, he took a final scroll through his email and fired off a message to Clare.

"How's your week going?" he wrote. "Any plans to visit? I wish you lived a little closer. You could always move back to New Jersey and work for your old man. I bet you'd make a great financial advisor." Max knew Clare had no interest in the investment business, but he figured she'd appreciate the sentiment.

He checked the markets one last time. The stock and bond markets were holding steady, but gold had slipped a little and was now at $1,650. It looked like it would be a quiet day in the markets, so not many clients would call. Alison should have an easy afternoon.

He headed down the street to the parking lot. Despite dilly-dallying in the office, he had still left ridiculously early. The hotel was only 20 minutes away and he had given himself 45 minutes to get there. He dawdled a little, checking out the other pedestrians, paying particular attention to men of his age, those in their late 40s and early 50s. They were an uninspiring bunch, their faces a little puffy and their shirts straining outward at the gut.

Max decided the contrast was all in his favor. He was lean, maybe too lean. His exuded a sense of good health. There was a bounce to his step. He had never considered himself much more than average looking. But maybe his moment had finally arrived. He was gaining on his male competitors, if only because others were dropping by the wayside. Maybe he shouldn't be surprised that a woman like Sara would choose him.

"Yeah, you really are an egotistical son-of-a-bitch," he chuckled to himself.

It was a battle against our instincts that we all fought. Max saw it in his business. Managing money was simple. But it wasn't easy. With a little effort, his clients could quickly learn the rudiments of managing a portfolio and save themselves a truckload of money. After all, if someone had a $1 million portfolio, Max's one percent fee worked out to $10,000 a year. Problem was, most people couldn't stare down their own demons. They knew they should sit tight when the market fell and maybe even buy more, and yet their inclination was to panic and sell.

Similar battles raged throughout our daily lives.

Folks knew they shouldn't eat so much, and yet they did. They knew they should exercise more, but they didn't. They were determined to spend less and save more, and yet month after month they failed. We thought we had free will, Max mused, but maybe we were just a bundle of hard-wired instincts, some good, some bad, that we invariably caved into.

Of course, with his new-found devotion to exercising, it looked like he had his instincts firmly under control. But maybe he was just driven by a different set of instincts. He was looking for a new mate. Like a male peacock, he needed the plumage to attract a female. Shedding 20 pounds might look like remarkable self-discipline. But maybe it was just a primitive attempt to make himself appear like a desirable mate.

He unlocked the car, fired up the engine and smiled at the afternoon ahead.

In Greenwich, Conn., a hedge-fund manager stared at the computer screen and ate his lunch without tasting it. He had bet $30 million on gold at $1,700 and now it was at $1,650. That was just a three percent decline, nothing more than a market belch. Problem was, he hadn't simply bought $30 million of gold. Rather, he had borrowed heavily and bought complex gold-linked securities, so his bet on gold was closer to $1 billion. That meant the three percent decline had wiped out his $30 million investment.

That was significant, but not terrible. The fund had other investments that were holding up just fine. But the gold market's decline was creating three additional headaches. First, the bank was asking for more collateral because of the shrinking gold position. Second, his fund's trading desk was hearing that other hedge funds were whispering about his losses. Finally, June 30 had just passed and clients were about to get their quarter-end reports showing the large stake in gold. Soon they would be calling—and he wanted to be able to tell them the gold was gone. Selling $1 billion of gold was no small task. It was so easy to amass these big positions and so difficult to unload them. He felt a tightening in his chest. He had foolishly boxed himself in. Years of playing the market told him he should get out. This could be messy.

"Charlie," he barked down the phone to his head trader. "Try to make it orderly. Try not to panic the market. But close out the gold position and let's get it done by the end of the week."

Fifteen minutes later, $40 million of gold hit the market. The price dropped to $1,640, but then bounced back to $1,642. Half an hour later, $30 million more followed. The price slid to $1,635, paused briefly and then dropped another $10.

"What the hell is happening?" The hedge-fund manager stood by the trading desk, leaning over his head trader. Both of them studied the computer screen like they were trying to divine some hidden message. "The market shouldn't have any problem absorbing this amount of selling."

"We clearly aren't the only ones trying to sell," said Charlie. "Things don't look good. I don't like the way the market's acting."

"We just got another call from the bank," came a shout from across the trading room. "They're demanding more collateral. And they don't sound happy."

The hedge-fund manager stood stoically, absorbing the blow and resisting the urge to release a string of expletives. He took a deep breath, and felt the dampness spreading from his armpits and soaking his shirt.

"Okay, boys, listen up," he said, his voice quieter than before and yet commanding the attention of everybody in the room. "We're going to call every goddamn dealer in every goddamn market in every goddamn continent. Spread it around, $20 million here, $30 million there. But get the gold sold. Today."

"Gold dropped $212 in frenetic trading," intoned the news show anchor. "Regulators in Washington are investigating what triggered the selloff. At least three hedge funds suffered massive losses, and have announced their intention to liquidate and return whatever money remains to investors. Today's gold-market collapse was the largest one-day decline in history. It has many experts asking, 'Is the great gold bull market over?' The decline spilled over into the stock market, with the Dow Jones Industrial Average dropping 342 points. Traders said some investors were selling stocks to cover their losses in the gold market. As the gold and stock markets fell, it triggered a flight to safety, with many investors moving money into the bond market. Bond prices rose sharply as the yield on the benchmark ten-year Treasury note fell from 3.42 percent to 3.18 percent."

A retired aerospace engineer stared at the TV in his Paris hotel room, listening as CNN recounted the day's events. The stock market had only just closed in

New York, but it was past 10 p.m. in France. He had a stomach full of fine French food. He felt sick. He stared at his sleeping wife and fought the urge to blame her.

In New York, a young advertising account executive heard the news on the office television. She went slightly pale, eased her way out of the crowd that surrounded the TV and headed back to her cubicle. There, she logged onto her 401(k) plan and sold her three growth-stock funds. "Thank God I never told my parents," she whispered to herself.

At a house closing in Atlanta, a young couple was happily agreeing to 30 years of mortgage payments that would put them back $1,826 every month. Her BlackBerry was switched off. That meant she didn't see the email from her boss at the event-planning firm she worked for, saying he wanted to talk to her about her hours. When the stock market declined, rich folks got scared and stopped holding big parties. Business was likely to be slow. He would need to take a close look at costs.

Alison was also watching the news. It had been an exhausting afternoon. As the stock and gold markets plummeted during the afternoon, she had fielded concerned calls from eight clients, with no help from Max. From reading his emails, she knew exactly where he was. She was almost tempted to phone the hotel and tell him to get his increasingly skinny ass back to the office.

From reading his emails, she also knew about the message he'd sent to Clare earlier in the day. Was he serious? Did he truly want Clare to move back home and work for him? The more Alison brooded over the possibility, the more incensed she became. Would he really consider turning over the business to his oldest daughter after the years Alison had spent sweating away in this wretched suite of offices in suburban New Jersey, giving her all to make sure Whitfield Financial was a success?

She had dreamt and daydreamed about owning the firm. She had savored the sense of triumph she'd feel when she told her parents that she had her own money-management business. But now everything was in jeopardy. Max couldn't be trusted to run the business the right way. He couldn't be trusted to reward her for all her hard work. He was just mooching off her talent while he ran around doing whatever the hell he wanted.

It was time she took matters into her own hands. The gold-market collapse was going to make things more difficult. Investors would no longer be so dissatisfied with their portfolio's performance. But she had ammunition. She had Max's inattention to clients to use against him—as well as ample evidence of his infidelity.

While Sara poured more champagne, Max snuck a quick look at the financial news. He hoped Alison hadn't been inundated with calls. The stock-market losses would unhinge some clients, but at least they would make back part of their losses with their bonds. The good old balanced portfolio of stocks and bonds had once again proven its worth.

More important, none of his clients owned gold. Or, at least, he hadn't bought any for them. Who knew what they might have done with other money they had? Max couldn't help but feel smug. Wall

Street excesses eventually correct themselves, but rarely did gratification come so quickly and so decisively.

"Sorry to be watching TV," he said. "But this is sort of a big deal for my business."

"That's okay. I think it's cool you know so much about managing money. Someday, maybe you could help me with my finances."

"I'd be happy to do it."

"Things are sort of a mess. My ex was a financial disaster and I should have paid more attention. I have some savings. But I only just finished paying off my half of the credit-card debt, most of which was used for stuff he bought, golf clubs, video games, a new paint job for his car, stupid stuff like that."

Max gave her the kindly, understanding look he had perfected for clients who had got themselves into financial difficulty. "Don't fret about it," he said. "Really. With a little time, you'll be back on track. In any case, I have more than enough money for both of us."

He reached up and stroked her cheek, only to see storm clouds rolling across her face.

"What's wrong?" Max's voice was filled with anxiety.

"Nothing."

"What is it?"

"Nothing, just nothing. I don't want to talk about it. Okay?" Sara struggled to put the moment behind her.

"Okay," said Max, feeling anything but.

She grabbed his face with both hands, silencing him with a long kiss. "You're a lovely man," she whispered. He felt her hand run down his chest and his confusion gave way to arousal. He returned her kiss and began to explore her body once again.

Some mornings, he wanted to ride. But some days, he needed to. Today was that sort of day. In search of clarity, others might pray or meditate or take long walks. For Max, suffering on the bicycle had come to serve that purpose. He needed to clear his head.

He had never been especially comfortable in the company of men. He squirmed amid the crass comments about breast size and who they'd like to screw. He much preferred women.

But this was overkill. He felt surrounded. There was Alison at the office, his daughters on the phone, Karen at home and Sara whenever he could see her. He would have been happy to sit in silence with any one of them. But they all wanted to fill the silence with talk. It was exhausting.

Karen alternated between excessive kindness and probing questions about where he had been, who he had seen and what he was doing on the computer. She asked him whether he thought Alison was attractive. She asked him whether he thought any of his women clients were particularly good looking. The questions he understood. She must sense he's having an affair. But what was with the excessive kindness? She asked if he was lonely. She fretted about his weight loss. She asked if everything was okay at work. It was almost as if she were the guilty one. Max wondered when bitchy Karen would return. She, at least, had a comforting air of familiarity.

And he wondered when bitchy Alison would depart and kindly Alison would return. She used to be so sweet. But now she complained bitterly about her workload, about his absences, even throwing in derogatory comments about men being pigs. Had she broken up with her boyfriend? Had there been a boyfriend? Max couldn't recall.

But Sara was the real mystery. They had wonderful times together, lovemaking like he couldn't recall. Yet, again and again, she closed down on him, just at the moment when he felt they were getting really close. Did she truly love him?

People were a package deal, that he knew. Mixed in with the wonderful qualities would always be stuff that was irksome. Years of marriage had taught him that. But Max never found Sara irksome. He found her an enigma. He wondered whether there was something she wasn't telling him. Had her ex been abusive? Was she that scarred by her marriage? Max felt like he was missing some crucial piece of information.

Only his daughters seemed unchanged. Melanie was as absent as ever. Clare was as sweet as always. He would have loved to have talked to Clare about all that was rolling around in his head, about Sara, about both the joys of the relationship but also his concerns. But, of course, he couldn't. There was nobody he could talk to. It was a secret affair. If he started blabbing, it wouldn't be a secret anymore.

So he hunched over the handlebars and pounded the pedals. It was going to be a busy few days at the office. This morning, he needed to be on time.

"No, you don't own any gold," he patiently explained to Mrs. Deveney. "Yes, there are stocks in your portfolio and they've been dragged down by all the panic selling. But you aren't losing nearly as much as the stock-market averages, thanks to the money you have in bonds."

Max had lost clients as the market rose. Now, there was a risk he would lose clients as the market fell. When markets were climbing, giddy investors would want to take on even more risk. But that courage quickly evaporated when prices fell. From years of experience, he knew many clients would now be desperate to sell stocks.

Still, Max felt back in control. This was familiar territory. The earlier obsession with gold was a craziness that defied rationality. But he had seen market declines like this before.

"You should be growing more enthusiastic, Mr. Cameron, because stocks are now better value. Even as the market is tumbling, the economy is still growing. You're right, there is a risk of recession, but the indicators suggest we won't get one. If the economy continues to expand, that should drive up corporate profits, which will allow companies to reinvest in their own business and also return money to shareholders by paying bigger dividends and buying back shares. Eventually, investors should recognize the value that's being created and they'll bid up share prices."

He would talk to clients about how their stocks weren't just ticker symbols and notations on their quarterly account statement. "As a shareholder, Mr. De Jong, you're a beneficiary of all the improvements that are occurring in the real economy. Unless you think the economy is going to collapse and never recover, the stock market should come back. Rough times like this are the price we pay to earn decent returns."

With his clients who were still in the workforce, he would remind them that it would be years, and often decades, until they would need to sell stocks and tap their portfolios for income. They still had their human capital—their ability to pull in a paycheck—to pay the bills.

Meanwhile, he would remind retired clients how much they had in bonds. He would then compare the value of their bonds to how much income they needed each year from their portfolio. "Mike, thanks to all the money you have in bonds, you could go ten years without selling any of your stocks," he told Mr. Davies.

Max delivered these little pep talks again and again. It had been just over a week since the gold market had come unglued. He had talked to all 72 of his clients. No one had bolted or demanded he sell stocks. He could hear the relief on the other end of the phone. Max had been doing this a long time. This he was good at. He felt like an athlete performing at his peak potential or a musician giving an especially fine concert, when everything seems to come together at just the right moment.

He put down the phone, leant back in his chair and raised his arms above his head, as if crossing the finishing line in triumph. Friday evening had finally arrived. He drank in the sense of accomplishment. It had been years since he had felt this energized by work.

He had tomorrow's group ride to look forward to. It would be one of those stinking hot early August days. He would enjoy sitting in the saddle, sweating and suffering, putting behind him the pressures of the work week. If he got his chance, he'd throw down the gauntlet at the end and see if he could once again blow the group apart. He also had next week's rendezvous with Sara. He imagined the fun of spending a few hours exploring her body and bringing her to orgasm. Life was good.

"Have a great weekend," he said to Alison as he headed out the door. "We did good this week. I don't know about you, but I'm going home and I'm going to have a great big glass of red wine."

"You fucking asshole. You fucking asshole. I can't believe you did this. You fucking asshole."

Thirty minutes earlier, Max had left the office. But instead of the relaxing Friday evening with a few glasses of wine, he walked into the house and was engulfed by Karen's fury.

"After 25 years, 25 fucking years, you do this. You asshole. Who is this woman? How dare you? How dare she?"

Max tried to remain calm, summoning the same mental toughness that had helped him keep clients on track during the past week's market craziness. But the questions were piling up in his head. He had sensed Karen was suspicious. But how had she found out? What did she know? Had she seen the credit-card bills? Had she got into his email? Had one of their friends spotted him with Sara? Did she know who Sara was and where she lived?

"What the fuck have you got to say for yourself?" This was delivered at a pitch that made Max wonder whether the neighbors were also learning of his infidelity.

In these situations, he often favored silence, waiting for the storm to pass. But it was pretty clear this storm wasn't passing.

"I'm sorry," said Max. "I'm truly sorry."

"So you admit it. It is true."

That threw Max. Did Karen know for sure or didn't she? With his apology, had he just shot himself in the foot? He looked at Karen and nodded.

"So what the fuck has been going on?"

Max had never heard Karen use the word "fuck" so often. It struck him as a little excessive. Earlier generations would have been appalled to hear a middle-aged woman use such language. So uncouth.

All right, Max counseled himself, maybe I'm focusing on the wrong issue here.

"I said, what the fuck has been going on?"

Okay, that's the issue I should be focusing on. But what do I say? How do I respond without making things even worse? Does Karen really want to know the gory details of every rendezvous with Sara? Does she already know?

Max puffed out his cheeks and exhaled. And that's when it struck him: He really didn't care if it got worse. So he said it: "I don't love you."

Karen looked like she had been slapped. Max was impressed. He hadn't given the words much thought. He just plucked them out of the air, opened his mouth and out they came. Yet he managed to utter the one phrase that cut to the heart of the issue, short-circuited the conversation—and ended his marriage.

"Fuck you," Karen screamed. There was the "fuck" word again. Max was pretty sure the neighbors heard that one. "Get the fuck out of the house. You'll be hearing from my fucking lawyer."

"You've already hired a lawyer," Max wanted to say.

But he decided that probably wouldn't be a helpful comment, so he held his tongue, walked down to the basement, grabbed two suitcases and headed to the bedroom. He figured he had better snag what he needed now, because he probably wouldn't get another chance any time soon.

Karen watched Max's car pull out of the driveway, the backseat full of clothes and his beloved bicycle on a rack hanging off the back. She had done it. For months, she had been mulling it over, wondering how she could transform her life once and for all, how she could make that final mental break from her old life of carpooling kiddies, suffering through school concerts and making healthy lunches. She had worried about the pain she might cause Max.

But then it turned out his tacky assistant was a loose-lipped turncoat and, with astonishing suddenness, all her problems were solved. She had to give Charles his due. He had been right. He had been the first to suggest that Max was having an affair.

Karen thought she would feel victorious, that it would be a great cathartic moment, that berating Max would let her unleash years of mounting frustration. But instead, she felt soiled. Maybe it was because she knew she was no innocent. Maybe it was because her hand had been forced, rather than her getting to decide when and how their marriage ended. Maybe it was because she had no desire to spend the rest of her life with Charles. Probably it was the "I don't love you."

There was a finality to it. She knew there would be no reconciliation. She could tell Max didn't want it. She was pretty sure she didn't, either.

The breakup may have just happened, but it was clear they had parted ways months and maybe years earlier. Karen felt sad, not so much because her marriage was over, but because the relationship that once promised to be her life's defining thread had now become so tawdry. Back in her early 20s, she thought they would be making gooey eyes at each other for the rest of their lives. Instead, they ended up not hating the other, but with something far worse: indifference.

Her heels clicked down the empty hallway to the study. She took a long pull on her scotch and water, grabbed the Yellow Pages and started looking up attorneys.

Max sat in the motel room, his laptop resting on his knees, trying to locate the free wireless access. He had picked up a bottle of red on the drive over, realized he didn't have a corkscrew and had to make a second trip to the liquor store. He now had his big glass of wine. It didn't taste so good.

The motel was relatively new, probably built only five or six years earlier. It oozed impermanence. The wallboard had been slapped onto two by fours, covered with spackle and then painted a grim off-white. A single cheap print was tacked onto the wall above the bed. Max figured the building might last 20 years, 25 tops. If he died during the night, it would be the ultimate indignity, to be found lying between the thin sheets and under the skimpy blanket, his head on the rubbery pillow. He hated to think what germs lay encrusted on the hideous polyester bedspread. Maybe that would be the source of his untimely demise.

Max had tried to call Sara, but she hadn't picked up. Had Karen found her number and called her? Max hoped not. Did Sara say she was going out tonight? He didn't recall her saying so, but maybe it had slipped his mind. He decided not to leave her a message. Whatever he said to the machine would, he knew, be secondary to the tone of his voice, and he wasn't sure the tone would be right. So he decided to write an email.

He had initially convinced himself that his relationship with Sara was potentially one-sided, that single Sara needed him more than married Max needed her. But who was he kidding? He needed her desperately and never more so than now. He craved her presence and her affection. But he also knew that, if she realized how much he wanted her, it would drive her away.

Something wasn't quite right with their relationship. After the initial weeks, she never seemed that anxious to see him. They always met at her convenience, not his. She was in no great hurry to respond to his emails and she never seemed to initiate the correspondence. She often made cutting comments. Now that he was sitting alone in a motel room, with no need to go home to Karen, he realized it all with brutal clarity.

He wrote a simple factual account of what had happened, leaving out most adjectives and adverbs, and signed it, "Love, Max." With a sinking feeling, he hit the send button.

Alison wasn't sure she felt guilty. Guilt wasn't prominent among her range of feeling. But she clearly had some misgivings. Even as she delighted in telling her parents and her friends that she was now president and sole owner of Whitfield Financial Advisors, she couldn't quite bring herself to explain exactly how she had managed to persuade Max and Karen Whitfield to sell their 98 percent stake.

Still, while her behavior wasn't above reproach, her scheme was a thing of beauty. It started with a concerned call to Karen, saying she wasn't sure she should be doing this, but—one woman to another— she felt compelled to tell Karen that Max was straying from the straight and narrow.

To her surprise, Karen got a little snippy, said she had already suspected as much and gave the distinct impression that she didn't like receiving confirmation from her husband's junior assistant. She then demanded to know all that Alison knew. That led to an early morning meeting over coffee, where Alison showed her some of Max's emails. Karen took a glance at a few of the messages and then hurriedly handed them back. There followed another round of snippy questions, together with some pointed remarks about Alison's weakness in the ethics department. By the end of their meeting, Alison decided that she didn't really like Karen all that much and she could understand why Max was screwing around. But Alison kept such thoughts to herself.

Following their early morning coffee meeting, things moved quickly. On Saturday morning, Alison logged onto Max's email and read his matter-of-fact message to Sara, where he explained that he had been tossed out on his ear and that his marriage would soon be joining the unhappy half that didn't make it.

Alison then waited five days, out of some lingering sense of decency, before she called Karen again, this time to ask what she planned to do with her half of the 98 percent. After all, Max had launched and built the business after they were married, so it represented marital property and hence half rightfully belonged to Karen. Could she really trust Max to look after the business on her behalf? Wouldn't it make more sense to sell? Which is what Karen agreed to do.

That was followed by a conversation with Max, during which Alison explained that Karen had called, offering to sell her 49 percent stake in Whitfield Financial Advisors. Assuming all the details could be ironed out, Alison would soon own 51 percent of the firm. Would Max like to sell his 49 percent stake? Even Alison realized that compelling somebody to part with his business, especially one he had spent his entire adult life building, could trigger an angry reaction.

She sat in Max's office, in one of the two chairs facing his desk. She imagined her fingers in her ears, as she awaited the explosion. But in fact, Max seemed almost relieved. His life was spiraling downward and he was anxious to figure out where the bottom was, so he could start crawling his way back to daylight.

He looked Alison up and down, rubbing his hand across his unshaven face. "Three percent of assets," he said.

"Two percent," she countered.

"Okay, so we've agreed to two-and-a-half percent.

Clients have $65 million with us right now." Max grabbed a calculator. "That means you need to come up with $1.6 million, half of which goes to me and half to Karen. Deal?"

"Deal."

"You've got two weeks to borrow the money. I'll have my attorney send over the contract." With that, Max stood up, muttered a quiet "fuck my life" and walked out of the offices of Whitfield Financial Advisors for the last time.

Karen wandered from room to room, as if looking for something she had lost. But in truth, she was just looking, trying to find her bearings in a place that was both familiar and disorienting.

Melanie and Clare's bedrooms were strangely antiseptic, as though all the personality had been drained out of them. Maybe it was just the absence of dirty clothes on the floor. Max's study looked liked a room abandoned ahead of an approaching tornado, with everything in its place except the few precious possessions he had grabbed on his way out the door. The closet in the master bedroom had a yawning gap where his clothes used to hang. Karen had resisted moving some of her clothes into the space. She wasn't sure why.

She had also resisted Charles's suggestion that he come over. It felt wrong. The family that once lived here may have been torn apart. But Karen could still recall the bustle and the banter. Charles was never a part of that. He would be an intruder, stomping on memories he knew nothing about.

She could have gone to Charles's house this

evening. In recent weeks, she had done that every night. It wasn't so much that she wanted to be with Charles. She just didn't want to be here. But tonight, she decided to bite the bullet and confront the strangeness of her own home. Could she ever live here again? Should she sell?

Once the divorce was final, Karen would be rich and single. She still had a few years until she turned 50. It was hard to sort through all the possibilities. Should she stay in the house, move to a smaller place in town, move into the city or maybe move to another part of the country? She was liberated from the three responsibilities that had weighed so heavily on her just a few years ago. There was no more worrying about what to feed Max, Melanie and Clare for dinner. There were no more dental appointments to arrange, no more beds to change, no more shopping trips to clothe them.

Her anger at Max had quickly waned, though the sense of betrayal still stung. Partly, it was the shock of learning that he, too, had been unfaithful. Had there been other women? How long had their marriage been a fraud? She looked back, wondering whether there were signs she had missed.

But it was more than just the surprise. Karen felt cast aside. Yes, she wanted a new life. But she never saw Charles as a replacement for Max. Rather, Charles was an experiment, a tentative step as Karen tried to figure what her new life might look like and whether it was the life she wanted. But there was nothing tentative about Max's actions: He had clearly thrown her aside in favor of this Sara woman.

She mused that she might have felt better if she had been the one caught, and Max the one left confused and scrambling to make sense of it all. But as best she could tell, Max knew nothing of Charles, so he wouldn't have any feelings of rejection. Only she knew the entire story—of her betrayal of Max, Max's betrayal of her, Alison's betrayal of Max.

She was almost tempted to tell him about her affair, so he too would know that he had been less than his spouse had wanted. Karen certainly felt inadequate: From her quick look at the emails Alison had purloined, she knew that Max had found somebody who excited him in a way she no longer could. Judgment had been rendered. Karen has been deemed undesirable. She had joined the ranks of middle-aged women who had been left behind.

Clare phoned frequently, anxious to check that her mother was okay. Karen took to avoiding her calls. She suffered no pangs of guilt over her affair with Charles, except when Clare phoned and offered a sympathetic ear. She felt like she had been unfaithful not to Max, but to the motherly image she had so carefully cultivated with her daughters.

Of course, at this juncture, she could tell Clare, Melanie and everybody else about Charles and fib that the relationship had started after Max had moved out. But if anything, she was now more fearful of being discovered. What would people think? Karen may have been older than Charles, but she considered herself a decent catch. Nobody would claim that for Charles. He was verging on the rotund and he was a little rough around the edges, always inclined to make the remark that bordered on the inappropriate. Karen lived in fear of what might come out of his mouth next. How had he ever ended up as head of human resources?

It was one thing to revel in the secret pleasure of her affair with Charles. It was another matter to play it out in public. Indeed, as her anger and distress had ebbed in recent weeks, her relationship with him stood out like a rock revealed by the receding tide. He had become a larger part of her life than she had ever intended and he was set to become a larger presence still, her constant companion at the office, at home, in public. As she contemplated the prospect, waves of anxiety washed over her.

So she told Charles that she wanted to keep their relationship quiet for now, at least until the divorce was wrapped up. She explained that she didn't want to anger Max and make negotiating a property settlement more fraught. It could also derail her promotion. Charles readily agreed.

Karen had bought herself time to think.

He spun the pedals easily, drifting down the road. This was meant to be his long Saturday ride, but he didn't have the heart or the legs for it. It had been five weeks and a day since Karen had pronounced him a "fucking asshole." Until that moment, he had been a moderately prosperous financial advisor with all the trappings of suburban success. Now, he was unemployed and holed up in a dingy apartment he rented month-to-month.

He certainly wasn't poor. After selling his business, signing over the house to Karen and splitting the assets they had, he would have around $2½ million. But he was finding it hard to feel fortunate.

How had he ended up here? When had the spiral downward begun? How had it unraveled so quickly?

Max wondered when the turning point had occurred. Had there been a fork in the road where, unbeknownst to himself, he had made a crucial choice? Maybe it began when he hauled his father's old bike out of the garage. When he hurriedly moved out, he had left his Dad's bike behind. Would Karen throw it out? Would she do that to him?

Or maybe the unraveling started the day he talked to that woman in the delicatessen. No, not Sara. The previous woman. What was her name? Max wasn't sure he ever knew it. But he could still vaguely remember her face. She had a birthmark, Max recalled, right above her lip.

Perhaps it began when he started letting Alison assume more responsibility at Whitfield Financial Advisors. Initially, he had presumed that he had been undone by his own carelessness, that maybe subconsciously he had wanted to get caught. It had taken him weeks to figure out that there was no self-sabotage, that Alison had ratted him out to Karen. How could he have been so naïve, so clueless? Even after Alison had bought Karen's share and then offered to buy his, it didn't twig that she was the one behind his marriage's collapse.

He had lost his wife. Okay, that didn't seem like much of a loss. He was astonished how infrequently he thought of Karen. It could be his heartlessness, but he preferred to think it was a reflection of how much their relationship had deteriorated. He knew he loved her once. But amid 25 years of mowing lawns, buying groceries and supervising homework, that love had got misplaced. Max, for one, had no idea where to find it.

Still, the familiarity of home was gone and his daily

routine had been upended, and he missed those elements of his old life. He missed the ringing of the phone and discovering Clare on the other end. He missed slipping into his chair at the office and assuming command of Whitfield Financial Advisors. He missed wandering out at lunchtime to grab a sandwich or a few slices of pizza. He felt a little untethered. He had tried to build a new routine in his new apartment. He was frequenting the same coffee shop, the same grocery store and the same pizza place on a regular basis. But he felt like a clumsy alien invading somebody else's world.

It didn't help that he had nowhere to go during the work week. Should he blame himself for losing the business? Max pondered the question. As the business reached the point of modest prosperity, he could have settled back and collected one fat paycheck after another. He had always thought that was the goal. But comfortable success wasn't enough. Many days were almost too easy. Work was no longer a challenge.

He had asked Alison to take on more of his duties, telling himself that he was helping her hone her skills. But maybe, in truth, he just didn't want to do the work himself. Even when he was losing clients and it was clear his business was struggling, he couldn't stir himself to hunt for new customers or make much effort to placate those he still had. If there was any self-sabotage, it occurred not at home, but at the office.

With the sale of Whitfield Financial Advisors, he had lost much of his identity. He had also lost his regular income. When he owned the business, he had been able to retain some perspective on his wealth and his income, realizing that his financial success had hinged on a large element of luck. Life was an economic lottery and he had been on the winning end. At another time or in another society, his skills might have earned him nothing more than a pauper's wage. He just happened to have a set of skills—understanding the markets, being able to connect with clients—that had brought him a healthy income.

But, of course, it's easy to be philosophical when you're on the winning end. The fact was, the lottery had now stopped paying and he wasn't exactly feeling philosophical. He missed the income, not so much for the raw dollars, but for the sense of security and privilege that came with it. Now all he had was a hefty pile of stocks, bonds and cash.

He also had Sara. Sort of. He had seen her twice every week since Karen had tossed him out, with a regularity more reminiscent of a dental appointment than a meeting of lovers. Their conversations were more stilted. There just wasn't that much going on in his life, so there wasn't much to say, no amusing anecdotes about clients, no keen insights into the markets.

Their lovemaking had also lost much of its passion. He started to notice odds things about her, like the thinness of her lips and the slightly distasteful smell of her breath. He no longer got lost in the moment. Now, even as he hurtled toward orgasm, he found himself standing apart, analyzing her and picking through their relationship.

As Max talked about the breakup and what he might do next, Sara was attentive and mostly kind, but also distant. Max couldn't quite put his finger on it. She would be loving toward him one moment, cracking a joke at his expense the next. He yearned to see her more and recapture the intensity of their relationship's early days, and he knew he didn't hide his desperation well. They could have been building a new life together.

Maybe she would come around. Maybe. But he had that terrible sense that this was not a relationship of equals, that he was fonder of her than she was of him, and that only made him more desperate. The scent of death hung over the relationship and he hadn't a clue what to do about it.

So what did Max have left? He was sitting on it. The bicycling was the only part of his old life that was still intact, and yet here he was on a Saturday morning puttering along, allowing the disarray in the rest of his life to sully his one remaining pleasure. He pulled over to the side of the road and checked the bicycle computer: 31 miles at 18.7 mph.

"I know, I know, it's pathetic," he spoke to the handlebars. "Sorry, you deserve better." He zeroed out everything on the computer and set off again, this time cranking the pedals for all he was worth.

FALL

O n warmer days, the bicycle would dance through the dry leaves, scattering them in all directions. It reminded Max of his childhood, walking to school with friends and kicking leaf piles along the way.

On wetter days, he rode with a little less abandon, taking the corners more tentatively, anxious to avoid skidding on the soggy leaves and on the painted white lines that divided the road from the hard shoulder. Still, if anything, he enjoyed it more when the days were wetter and colder. He took pride in his toughness, getting sweaty and dirty in the sloppy weather. He imagined slothful neighbors looking up from their flat-screen televisions and admiring him as he barreled past.

But did his neighbors really admire him? Or did they think he was some sort of nut? Max eyed the bicycle wearily. "Maybe we'll make it a shorter outing today." He contemplated a trio of possible routes, all around 20 miles. How many times had he ridden those routes over the past two months? Every other day? Maybe more?

"Oh, that's right, we did a shorter ride yesterday. I guess we ought to do a 40-miler." He hauled the bicycle onto his shoulder and carried it across the living room carpet to the apartment's front door, his thoughts drifting to the burger and fries he might buy afterwards to reward his efforts.

When Max still had a job, he had been limited to long rides of two to three hours on Saturdays and Sundays and maybe three or four midweek morning rides of 40 or 50 minutes each, with the occasional evening ride after work. Every minute on the bicycle seemed precious and he dreamed of having more time to cycle.

But now, there were no restrictions on how much he could ride, except the restrictions imposed by his aging 48-year-old body. And his body wasn't imposing many restrictions. The accumulated miles had left him with a wiry toughness. As he lay in bed at night, he could feel his body's leanness. Liberated from the heat and humidity of summer, Max found himself cycling faster and farther. His bicycle computer attested to his increasing speed.

But while riding had never been so easy, it often felt like a grind. Some days, he couldn't wait for the familiarity of the saddle and the pleasure of whipping down the road. But today, as on many recent days, he could barely get himself out the apartment door, even though the ride was often the only notable event in his day. Therein lay the problem: He had too much time. Now that he could ride all day, bicycling didn't seem nearly so important or special. He was spinning his wheels for no reason.

He needed a reason. He needed his daily rides to be more meaningful. He needed a goal. What he needed, he realized, was a race.

The idea struck him mid-ride and his stomach immediately started to churn. Over the past five or six months, he had thought occasionally about racing. Sometimes, it had seemed daunting. Sometimes, it had seemed like a romantic undertaking. Now, as he noodled the idea and it blossomed into a real possibility, his reaction was unvarnished terror.

He knew he had to do it.

Back home, festering in his damp spandex shorts, he turned on his laptop and started scouring the Internet. The pickings were slim. It seemed the racing season was almost over. He found a couple of races listed for the final weekend of September and a smattering through October. There was even one race listed for the first Saturday in November. He clicked on the link.

It was a smalltime affair, four circuits of a moderately hilly ten-mile loop out in the New Jersey countryside, fairly close to the Pennsylvania border. It was organized by the local YMCA, some sort of fund raiser for its scholarship program. There were trophies for the top three male and female riders, but no prize money, so the professionals wouldn't bother. Frankly, it didn't look like the sort of race that would attract serious amateurs, let alone serious amateurs with a penchant for doping. You didn't even need a racing license from USA Cycling. It was really more of an organized ride than a race.

Max was intrigued. No pros. None of the good amateurs. Rural location. Who the hell was going to turn up? Max liked the odds. He found the page for online registration and filled in his name, address and credit-card information. Then he hit submit and found himself staring nervously at the computer screen. What had he just committed himself to? Max had an overwhelming urge to wet himself.

"I signed up for a race," he said. "It's November 3, a Saturday. Forty miles. Out toward Phillipsburg. I hope you'll come."

"Sounds dangerous."

"Yeah, I'll probably kill myself." Max looked across the table and mugged a broad grin. Sara didn't smile back. She ignored the menu and fiddled with her cutlery.

Was this the day? Max had seen it coming for weeks. He saw Sara take a deep breath. She was preparing to speak. Yeah, thought Max, this is the day. Breaking up in a restaurant? They were already sitting down. The waiter would soon be over to take their order. Other diners were nearby. Couldn't she have picked a better time and place? Or did she deliberately pick it because he was less likely to cause a scene?

"Max, we need to talk. About our relationship. We're clearly struggling."

That was a pretty lame start, said Max to himself. But he didn't say anything to Sara. He was sorely tempted. His instinct was to make it easier for her by filling the vacuum with words. But why make it easier for her? Max figured he'd let her talk her own way out of this one.

"You're a beautiful man," she continued. "There are many things about you that I adore. I've really enjoyed our times together."

She paused. Max looked at her, his lips sealed. She's trying to soften me up before she delivers the knockout blow, he thought.

"It's been fun," she added.

He continued to stare and say nothing.

"Some great moments."

More silent staring from Max.

"I've really grown fond of you."

He braced himself.

"But you've got to understand, Max. If I truly loved you, I would never have got involved."

"What?" Max blurted out.

"Come on, we both knew it wouldn't last."

"We did?" Damn it, surmised Max, I'm clearly not very good at giving the silent treatment.

"Okay, I did. We were trying it out, seeing what it was like to start a new relationship, something neither of us had done in many years. But this is the rebound relationship and now it's time to move on and find the real thing."

"Rebound relationship? The real thing?"

"Haven't you ever read any of the women's magazines?"

Max gave her a blank look.

"Yeah, I guess maybe you haven't," Sara conceded. Another pause and then she started up again, but this time looking away, studying the pictures on the wall, the maitre d', the double swinging doors leading to the kitchen, just about anything but Max's face.

"There's somebody else. His name is John. Nothing's happened between us. I met him about the same time I met you. I've been interested in him for months. But I didn't want to get involved with him until I had my rebound relationship, which was you. And it has been wonderful, really wonderful. But it's time to move on."

Sara finally returned her gaze to Max, but all she saw was the back of his head as he strode out the restaurant.

As Max bicycled through town toward open country, he lightly pushed the pedals, replaying the tape of the past few months in his head. At first, he had thought that he and Sara were wildly, crazily in love with each other. But it turned out he was the only one who had been wild and crazy. While his head was swimming with thoughts of love, a house in the country and their new life together, she had been having an entirely different relationship, one so carefully calculated that Max found it hard to comprehend.

He recalled snatches of conversations. While he had been professing undying love and talking about their future, she had often kept him at bay. He recalled her unkind comments. He thought them sassy and playful at the time. Maybe they were simply unkind.

He had believed he had drawn her in with his charm and his new, athletic body. But it was a fantasy—his fantasy, a great love affair concocted entirely by him. All the time, she had been in the driver's seat. She had picked him out and encouraged him, not because she totally adored him, but because she didn't. She was drawn to him, not because she thought she could lure him away from his wife, but because she assumed she wouldn't. She had set the pace, deciding when and where they would meet. He was her rebound relationship. He was appealing because he didn't make her heart do back flips. He examined the asphalt ahead and saw his ego splattered across the road.

"What a fucking fool," he muttered to himself, loud enough that at least one pedestrian turned and stared at him with an aggrieved look on her face. "No, not you, lady," he added, this time to himself.

Had she already slept with John, whoever the hell he was? He knew Sara didn't love him, had never loved him, had used him. And yet the thought of her sleeping with somebody else tore at his insides. It wasn't jealousy. It was the twice-felt rejection, the fact that she was both scorning his bed and also climbing into another.

The breakup would have stung far less if she had wanted to spend one final night with him, so he knew that she still had some lingering fondness for him, that she still found him attractive, that the rejection wasn't total—and so he could have the chance to say "no" to her. How could she share herself with him and then turn around and so quickly do so with someone else? It felt like an insult to the very notion of what love should be.

He passed through the last of the traffic lights, saw open road ahead, put down his head and started to pound the pedals. The fury and indignation of the past few months poured out. Alison. Karen. Sara. But mostly he directed his anger at himself. What an idiot he had been. He had thought that he was special, that he could hold back time, that he could reinvent himself, that he could start anew at age 48. But all he had managed to do was screw up his life, with nothing to show for it but a shiny new bicycle and 20 pounds less on his gut.

A good tradeoff? Max waited for the tidal wave of regrets. But even in his distress, he wasn't convinced that he had chosen badly. Was he really better off than he was six months ago? Or was his lack of regret just some kind of self-defense mechanism, a little trick of the brain to stop his descent into utter despair? He wasn't sure. But whatever the truth, he couldn't imagine returning to the life he had before.

Max sat at the dining room table, an ice pack on his left knee and a calculator and pad of paper in front of him. He figured that, once he paid capital-gains taxes on the sale of the business, he would have around $2.4 million. He would need to buy a new home. He budgeted $500,000 for that, leaving him with $1.9 million.

No doubt that would seem like a huge sum to 99 percent of Americans. But Max was—or, at least, had been—a financial advisor. What would he have said to a 48-year-old with $1.9 million who wanted to retire? He imagined the lecture he might deliver: You could easily live another 40 years. You don't know what sort of bumps you'll hit along the way, including bad financial markets, high inflation, nursing-home costs, helping your kids financially. You need to be really cautious about drawing down your savings. Maybe you should start with a three percent withdrawal rate and then bump it up to four percent once you get into your 60s. On $1.9 million, that three percent worked out to $57,000 in income for the first year of Max's enforced retirement.

It was a heck of a lot less than the $350,000 he used to earn. Would he find himself worrying about money? Max pondered the question. You notice money the most when you don't have enough. It was sort of like good health. You took it for granted much of the time. It is only when you're sick that you truly appreciate how great it is to feel well.

Still, Max could live on $57,000 a year. Like his old clients, he and Karen had always been pretty careful with their money, spending far less than their income and socking away the rest. And now, it was just him, not him and Karen. He could keep his costs low, buy a cheaper car, eat out less, take less costly vacations and find a house with lower property taxes. With a little thrift, he would never have to work another day in his life.

But what would he do with himself? When he had his business, he hungered for free time, imagining how blissful it would be to linger over the morning newspaper or watch some mindless show on television. Yet it had been barely two months since he had walked out of Whitfield Financial Advisors for the last time and already he was restless and occasionally bored. In fact, he was shocked by how easily he got bored. An unscheduled 30 minutes became a source of dread.

He wasn't built for lounging around. He needed to fill his days with things that he thought were important, that he found challenging, that gave him a sense of purpose, that he was passionate about. He needed a reason to get out of bed in the morning. The biking and the upcoming race helped. But biking only accounted for an hour or two of each day. That still left another 15 or 16 hours to fill.

What was he going to do? He contemplated the calculator and pad of paper, sought inspiration and came up short. So he struck a bargain with himself: He would give himself until after the race to come up with a brilliant idea.

If that failed, he'd start building another financial advisory business. It felt like a cop-out, going back to what he had done before, and he worried that his enthusiasm would quickly wane. But it would also be a challenge, like it had been in his 20s, when he was starting out. As part of his deal with Alison, he had agreed not to solicit business from any of Whitfield Financial Advisors' clients for the next three years. It had been fun building the business the first time around. Maybe it would be fun again. Maybe the best guide to his future happiness lay in what had made him happy before.

The women in his life were gone. Except his daughters, of course. But since Karen had discovered his affair, Melanie called even less frequently, which meant pretty much never. She was, however, at least cordial. Not so Clare. She was pissed.

He would have loved to talk to her about what had happened. He would have loved to talk to somebody. To talk about the affair, how it had fallen apart and how, even now, he found the whole thing puzzling. But there was nobody he could talk to about Sara. Sara without the stupid fucking 'h.'

He had mentioned to Clare that he and Sara had broken up, thinking she would be happy that the source of all the trouble was out of his life. But if anything, that just made Clare even angrier. She would have been irked if Sara were still around. But she was also irked that she was gone, because it confirmed that all the anguish was over some brief, meaningless affair. Max couldn't win.

So he told her about his wretched apartment, joking about the recent cockroach sighting, the noisy plumbing and the weird neighbors. "Of course, the neighbors probably think I'm pretty weird too, because all they ever see is me walking in and out of the apartment in spandex shorts," he said. "This really is a horrible place. I can't wait to own my own home again."

And, of course, he talked to Clare about bicycling, which was pretty much the only thing left in his life that was interesting and that he could mention without irritating her. He got her to laugh when he recounted shaving his legs, a ritual among hardcore cyclists, about how the bathtub looked like it had been used by a gorilla undergoing chemo.

"Really, it's given me a whole new sympathy for women who shave their legs," said Max, "especially those who wait 48 years between shavings."

He also got her to laugh when he told her about his night sweats. If he had a hard workout but didn't eat enough afterwards, he would often wake up at night totally drenched, beads of sweat pooling on his chest.

"Usually, a guy has to go through menopause to experience that," he quipped. That also got Clare to laugh.

Max had a lot of time on his hands—including time to sharpen his one-liners.

He told Clare about his race preparations, the long rides twice a week to build endurance, the tempo rides to test his ability to maintain speed over 20 miles, the hilly courses to improve his climbing ability, the sprint repeats on a quiet road with little traffic, the morning stretching routine to increase flexibility and strengthen his stomach muscles. He talked about how he had gradually increased his mileage, so he was now riding more than 200 miles a week. He wasn't sure she found it all that interesting. But when he asked whether she would drive down from Boston to watch the race, she said yes.

It was just a stupid local bicycle race. It would be a motley collection of amateurs of decidedly mixed talent. Many would be looking simply to finish the 40 miles. Maybe only a few dozen had serious thoughts of winning. The results probably wouldn't even make the pages of the local newspaper. There was no fame or immortality to be had.

But then again, as far as Max was concerned, there was precious little immortality to be had, either in this world or any other. The United States had had 44 presidents. No doubt all thought they had achieved some measure of immortality, and yet today most Americans couldn't name all 44 and certainly couldn't tell you much about each.

Max wasn't religious or even vaguely spiritual. He sure wasn't doing this for His or Her greater glory or approval. But on the off-chance that God did indeed exist, Max was pretty confident any self-respecting supreme being wouldn't give a hoot about some local bike race.

Still, even if history, God and everybody else didn't care about this rinky-dink 40-mile race in Bumfuck,

New Jersey, Max cared. He cared deeply. He harbored dreams of winning, though he would scarcely admit them to himself, much less to anybody else. He imagined crossing the finish line, pumping his fist victoriously, spectators applauding, Clare watching. Maybe not intentionally, but he had become the aging weekend warrior who quits his job to train full-time. There were no excuses. The race wasn't another thing in his life. It had become his life. Max draped the thought across his shoulders and tried it on for size.

The result was important, he couldn't deny it. But the race, he felt, was the thing. Only one person could finish first, but maybe he could at least finish feeling triumphant. The race gave him a chance, however briefly, to be greater than himself. It wasn't immortality, but maybe it was an immortal moment, a snatch of time when he could show his true potential and prove he still had all the vitality of 30 years earlier. Maybe this would be one of those stories that Clare and Melanie would tell his grandchildren.

These were the sort of addled thoughts that coursed through Max's mind as he ripped himself inside and out through a final 60-mile ride before the race. For the sake of his confidence, Max didn't want this last long ride to go badly. He took the corners with reckless abandon. He ran red lights. He let it fly down hills. He tucked behind trucks and tried to draft off them. He screamed at his legs to pedal faster.

He could tell himself all kinds of stories about the race, about how it would play out, about whether he was ready or not. He could imagine winning, or being the first finisher over age 40, or posting a time that shocked even himself. But the bike computer didn't tell stories. It told the truth. As he hit the brakes outside his apartment and banged out of the pedals, the verdict was in: 60.8 miles at 20.3 mph.

"Thank you, thank you," he stammered, trying to catch his breath and running his hand along the frame. "You're a beauty, a real beauty." Max didn't know whether it would be enough to put him in the money. But he was pretty sure he couldn't ride much faster.

He had set two alarm clocks, even as he assumed he wouldn't sleep. But Max managed five solid hours, which he decided was enough. He slipped out of bed at 3:30 a.m., an hour earlier than necessary, and headed to the kitchen, where he tried to stuff down as much cereal and as many bananas as his nerves would allow.

To kill time, he turned on his laptop, scanned the news on the Internet and absorbed almost nothing. He checked the weather. It would be in the 50s with little wind. That was a plus. He often struggled when cycling in the wind. His churning stomach triggered three trips to the bathroom. He could feel his pulse was slightly elevated and his breathing shallow. Max was wired.

Antsy to get going, he hit the road at 5:30. He had planned to leave at 6, but he just couldn't sit around any longer. Almost immediately, he needed to go to the bathroom again. "God, you're turning into a four-year-old," he berated himself. "Grow up."

As he drove, Max felt like he was in one of those off-kilter dreams, like he didn't know how to handle a car and might crash at any moment. It was as if he were sitting in the passenger seat, watching himself, wondering who the driver was and whether he could be trusted with the wheel. The street lights seemed brighter and the outlines of the trees and the houses were sharper. It was as if he were seeing things for the first time. Max was definitely wired.

The race didn't start until eight. He figured most people wouldn't be there until seven. But to his surprise, when he pulled into the parking lot at 6:35, there was already a slew of cyclists milling around in the semi-darkness.

Some were cruising the road, warming up their legs, while a few had their bikes set up on trainers and were spinning away. There were so many loud riding jerseys screaming the names of professional cycling teams. So many expensive bikes. Bianchi, Cannondale, Cervelo, Colnago, Felt, Fuji, Giant, Litespeed, Look, Specialized, Trek. It was a fashion show of magnificent machines. Max felt intimidated.

What was he doing here? What did he know about bicycle racing? Who was he to imagine he could win when he'd never before entered a race? He didn't belong here. He could still sneak away and nobody would ever know. This was all a terrible, terrible mistake. A misunderstanding. It was Saturday morning, he was supposed to be picking up bagels and the newspaper for the family, he had taken a wrong turn and somehow ended up here. Honest.

"I am so screwed," he told the front and rear wheels as he neurotically checked the tire pressure one more time.

With the enthusiasm of a death row prisoner, Max locked his car and headed to the registration tent to pick up his number.

*

Alison hadn't slept well. It had been weeks since she had slept well. She sat at the kitchen table, her hands cupping a mug of strong coffee, the caffeine gnawing at the pit in her stomach. She wanted to puke.

Maybe it wasn't such a clever scheme. The first part had gone fine. She had to force Max to sell her the business, preferably at a low price. The price wasn't all that low, but she had got the business. It was hers. After six years of playing second fiddle to Max, she finally got what she wanted. She understood the biz inside and out. She knew the computer systems and the clients. She had listened carefully to Max over the years. She might not have his intuition. But she had a pretty good grasp of how to manage money.

But things came unstuck when she turned to the second part of the plan, which was getting clients to accept her as their new financial advisor. It was the same in meeting after meeting. The retirees were especially scathing. "How old are you?" they'd ask. "Weren't you Max's receptionist? What happened to Max?"

She would talk about how Max had started coming into the office late and had been taking long lunches. She would explain that his wife had caught him cheating with another woman, that Karen had demanded a divorce and that Max had been compelled to sell the business. Alison saw it all as a searing indictment. Max's clients didn't view it that way.

"A man cheats on his wife and he has to sell his business." Mr. Davies shook his head sadly. "Is that what the world has come to? Max is a good man.

Who cares if he was getting to the office a little later? Who cares if he was taking long lunches? He looked after my money. He saved me from the whole gold debacle. He'd call on my birthday. He was very kind after my wife died. He'd take me to lunch occasionally. He would phone when the market had a bad day to make sure I wasn't concerned. He was a friend. Tell me again: How old are you?"

Alison offered to show Mr. Davies some of the emails Max had written to Sara. He looked horrified. Mr. Davies moved his account. So, too, did 33 other clients. When financial advisors in the area heard that Max had sold out to some kid barely out of college, they descended on her clients like vultures. It didn't take much to persuade the clientele of Whitfield Financial Advisors to move their accounts.

Alison was down to 38 investors, who between them had $34 million in assets. At one percent a year, that was $340,000 in revenue. With her overhead and the monthly interest payments to the bank, Alison was losing money big time. And there was every likelihood that more clients would head for the door.

Forget the fabulous success Alison had predicted for herself. Forget building a $1 billion money-management empire. The world was rendering its judgment and, for the first time in her life, it wasn't going her way. Alison was getting bitch-slapped.

She heard her father's voice. "Now, Ali, see if you can try a little harder." She racked her brains for a solution, but knew there wasn't one. She recalled how desperately she wanted to own Whitfield Financial Advisors, how she thought it was all that stood between her and happiness. She remembered her boasts to her parents and her friends. She thought about the unpaid bills. Her body heaved with a bitter sob, letting out a gasp from somewhere deep in her chest. That sob brought on another sob, and soon tears were streaming down her face and into her coffee cup.

As Max spun his way toward the starting line, he saw Clare standing on the sidewalk, a cup of takeout coffee in one hand. She had come. Max hadn't seen her since he and Karen had separated. He pulled over to the side of the road and wrapped her in his arms.

"Thank you so much for being here."

"I wouldn't have missed it for the world."

"It means a lot to me," said Max, his voice laced with emotion.

Clare looked around. "I've never seen so many beautifully shaven legs in my life."

"It's quite a sight," said Max, also taking in the view.

"How are you?"

"Other than the fact that my legs feel like lead, my stomach is doing somersaults and I'm ready to unload my breakfast underneath the nearest bush, things are wonderful."

Clare unveiled a huge smile. "You'll do great, Dad."

At the starting line, Max snagged a spot just behind the first line of riders. "Here we go, girl." He gave the bike a couple of gentle pats. "Let's see what we've got."

He was sure he needed to pee again. Some local official was droning on about the important work done in the community by the YMCA. Shut up already, thought Max. "For God's sake," muttered a rider next to him. Max felt an instant kinship.

"Your starting signal will be a three count, followed by an air horn," announced a race official. "Are you ready? Three, two, one." The horn blared and 212 cyclists rolled forward, the clatter of shoes clicking into pedals filling the air.

"Time to lock and load," he heard one cyclist declare. Max got cleanly into the pedals and breathed a small sigh of relief. After months of thought and preparation, the moment had finally arrived.

He expected everybody to gun it, but the start was surprisingly sedate, so he hung back, watching to see how things would unfold. A kid with a flat-handlebar bicycle and baggy shorts zoomed up the right-hand side of the pack and grabbed the lead. He won't last long, thought Max. He doesn't even have a proper road bike with dropdown handlebars. Still, the other riders scurried to line up behind him. Max did the same, but he made sure he was a dozen or so riders back from the front.

Led by a police car, they headed down Main Street and out into the countryside. On either side of the road, race marshals held back cars that were trying to enter from side streets. Max risked a quick glimpse at his bicycle computer. They were up to 24 mph, but it felt easy for now, sitting in the draft. He grabbed one of his bottles and took a swig of Gatorade. He had to keep himself fueled up.

The spectators were easily outnumbered by the riders. But a few lined the road, shouting encouragement. Somebody held up a sign, but Max couldn't read it. The houses became less numerous and farther apart, and soon all he saw were open fields and a few disinterested cows.

The kid with the flat-handlebar bike drifted back and out of sight, his shoulders crunched over and his face red with exertion. Max was now sitting eleventh.

It had been a hell of a week. Karen lay in bed, recalling the gory details with the trepidation of a hung-over partygoer who isn't sure she wants to remember everything that happened the night before.

On Thursday morning, she had been summoned to see the chief operating officer. His administrative assistant had called to say she was to be there immediately. Karen was surprised, but figured it was about her promotion to Charles's deputy. She took the elevator up to the seventh floor, where the most senior employees had their offices, and walked meekly into the executive suite, furtively noting the names on the doors as she hunted for the COO's office. Once there, his administrative assistant directed her to a nearby conference room, where she found the COO and the firm's chief counsel waiting for her.

"We have disturbing news regarding the conduct of Charles Hastings," began the chief counsel, a severe woman whose hair was so tightly tied back that the hair follicles at the crest of her forehead seemed frozen in a silent scream. "It seems Mr. Hastings has been behaving in an inappropriate manner at the office. On Tuesday, he made sexual advances toward one of the junior employees in human resources. He asked her to work late and then, once the other employees had left, he tried to grab and kiss her. We talked to Mr. Hastings yesterday and he didn't deny it." The chief counsel's voice turned droll. "In fact, he seemed rather proud of himself."

The chief counsel then nailed Karen with a look that suggested she had additional information about the sexual dalliances of Charles Hastings, but that information wouldn't be forthcoming at this juncture. Karen blushed.

"As you might imagine, this isn't considered acceptable employee behavior, especially when that employee happens to be the head of human resources," continued the chief counsel, her upper lip developing a nasty curl. She added, almost as an aside, "Such behavior, of course, doesn't come as an entire surprise to some of us. He never seemed like the ideal candidate for the position." She let that thought hang in the air while her curled lip enjoyed a momentary quiver. "We understand your specialty is firing employees. Mr. Hastings's services are no longer required by the corporation. Please inform him and arrange for an expedited departure."

Karen wandered back to the elevator, humiliated. They knew. They knew all about the affair, about their lunchtime frolicking, about the unethical attempt to make her Charles's deputy and get her a pay raise. They were punishing her. The whole thing was mortifying, not least because her name would now be forever linked with the undesirable Charles Hastings.

She walked into Charles's office and closed the door behind her. "I've been told to fire you."

Charles took it with remarkable calm. He leaned back in his chair, giving off the relaxed air of a happy and prosperous cherub. "Sorry this happened," he said, not sounding at all sorry. "I know it was a little sordid, that it wasn't the right thing to do given that I'm involved with you. But I couldn't help myself."

"You're a stupid fuck."

Charles continued to smile inanely. "I thought, if Karen Whitfield finds me attractive, maybe other women do as well. I had to find out."

"A really stupid fuck."

"Yes, I guess I misjudged the situation." He chuckled to himself, recalling his lunge at the young female employee, and then brought himself back to the moment. "I presume we can continue to see each other."

Karen rolled her eyes. "No, my God, no," she said, giving her head a slow, mournful shake.

"Why not?"

"This isn't the time to talk, Charles. You need to pack up your personal possessions. It's standard rules: You have an hour to be out of your office. Security will be here in a moment to observe you."

The following morning, she was again summoned by the COO's administrative assistant. She was ushered into the same conference room, but this time only the COO was present. She sat down opposite him, grim-faced, determined to maintain her dignity.

"I know you worked closely with Charles for a number of years," he began. Karen breathed deeply, trying to calm herself. "I imagine yesterday was a difficult day for you. As you no doubt know, Charles wanted you appointed as his deputy. We very much appreciate all that you've done for the company, not just yesterday, but in your many years as a full- and part-time employee. The long and the short of it is, we would like to offer you the position of head of human resources."

Karen shuddered at the memory and pulled the sheet up around her neck. Was the promotion also part of her punishment? A year ago, if she had been told she would soon be director of human resources, she would have imagined herself ecstatic. A month ago, if she had been told she would be rid of Charles so easily, she would have been thrilled.

Yet now, all she wanted to do was climb into the shower, turn on the cold water and scrub the stench of success from her body. She had everything she dreamed of and it felt like the most horrifying of nightmares. Dear God, how could she have ever slept with Charles? Dear God, how could she have sunk so much of her hopes and dreams into the stupid company?

Despite all the loathing she now felt, she couldn't help but think that maybe Charles had it right, that maybe she should have been a little more cynical. The motivational posters, happy talk corporate memos, conference room birthday celebrations and 6 p.m. drinks at a local bar: It suddenly struck Karen as the thinnest of glosses, lipstick slapped on the pig to cover up the terrifying rawness of the financial pact.

Of course, Karen should have known that. After all, she thought bitterly to herself, my specialty is firing employees.

They were coming through town after their first ten-mile circuit, a sleek line of beautiful machines and whirling feet. Max thought he was still eleventh, but he couldn't be 100 percent sure. He tried to get a look at the situation upfront, but it was hard to see how many riders were ahead, except on turns and that was a dangerous time to be looking anywhere other than at the rider and the road right in front of you.

He also didn't know how many riders were behind him. He could see the shadow of a cyclist sitting on his wheel. There were likely others lingering back there, but he couldn't tell how many.

Even so, Max felt reasonably happy with how things were playing out. He hadn't been blown out the back of the pack. So far, he had handled the pace pretty easily. He also hadn't spent any time at the front, so he felt fairly fresh. His sense was that the first five or six riders were taking turns leading, though he wasn't entirely sure.

The danger was that the pace line might split or a few riders might try a breakaway, and he would be left behind. It was a calculated risk. He figured he was safe for now. They were still in the war of attrition, with the stronger riders waiting for the relentless pace to take its toll on those who were weaker.

As they shot down Main Street, he saw Clare and gave her a nod. "Go Dad," she hollered. He wondered how many of his fellow racers were also fathers and thought the shout was for them.

Three miles out of town, they hit the first of the two major hills they tackled on each circuit. On the first go-around, the two hills had been a scramble, the pace line splintering as cyclists charged up the hill, but Max had held his own.

This time was different. Drafting didn't matter much at the slower speed on the hills, so riders unglued themselves from the wheel in front and started hammering their way up the climb. Stronger riders stood up on their pedals and sprinted the lower part of the hill. This was the moment when the weak were revealed, and Max was one of them: He was no sprinter. Panic washed over him as riders flashed past.

It was almost like he was standing still. His legs felt okay. He wasn't out of breath. He simply didn't have the raw power that the others possessed.

As the climb continued to bite, the sprinting cyclists grew tired, sat down and started churning their way up the hill. That gave Max the chance to drag himself up to the pack. As they crested the hill, he figured he was back around eleventh place again. It had been an ugly moment, he knew that. For the first time in the race, he felt his confidence start to ebb.

The second hill came eight miles into the circuit. He approached it with dread. Don't freak out, he told himself. You've seen this movie before. It'll be okay.

Sure enough, the hammerfest broke out on the lower slopes and Max found himself losing touch with the lead group, only to pull himself back into contention as the climb continued. Still, as they passed through town at the end of the second circuit, Max was growing leery of his chances. He might be able to handle the pace on the flats. But the hills could break him. If he fell too far behind the pack on one of the climbs, he would never have the speed to rejoin the lead group. Despite the chilly November morning air, sweat started to roll down his cheeks.

Sara sat on the edge of the bed and looked at John, who was still asleep, his sour breath spewing across the sheets toward her. He should be awake, talking to her, holding her in his arms.

"I've had better," she thought to herself.

But it wasn't just the lovemaking that had disappointed. The whole thing had been a letdown. Had she thought about this moment for too long?

Were her expectations too high? This was about finding somebody to spend the rest of her life with. How could her expectations possibly be too high?

Her ex had told her he didn't want to marry. But she had decided that he was simply nervous and, in his heart, truly wanted to wed. John, meanwhile, didn't say much at all, except occasional comments about sports or what he'd like for dinner. She had attributed his silence to a quiet thoughtfulness. But maybe she had it all wrong. Maybe all she needed to do was listen to the words they spoke. Maybe her ex didn't want to marry and maybe all John truly cared about were sports and food. Perhaps there was no need for interpretation. Perhaps men were that simple.

She thought wistfully about Max. Maybe she never gave him a chance. She was so focused on trying to get it right this time around. She didn't want a second divorce to her name. The thought of another breakup was almost more than she could bear.

So she had taken her cues from her ex-husband. He had ruled their relationship. She may have cajoled him into getting married. But he was the one calling the shots, deciding to wed and unwed.

This time around, she was determined to be the one in control. She locked up her emotions and approached the whole thing almost clinically, like she was ticking off the boxes in one of those surveys in a women's magazine. First, you have your rebound relationship. You get the craziness out of your system, make the mistakes, get your head straight. After that, you move on to Mr. Right. Sure, you play hard to get. But you eventually let him in and then you ride his gratitude all the way to the altar.

How could she have been so simplistic about it all, so naïve? But she already had her answer: Her entire adult experience with men consisted of her ex, Max and John—a failed marriage and two flimsy affairs. She had substituted reading for real relationships. Pretty much everything she knew about men she had learned from those wretched magazines. They really were horseshit. She vowed never again to pick one up in the supermarket checkout line.

It was a vow she would break.

Sara looked again at John. She suddenly had an overwhelming desire to get him out of her townhouse. She had got what she thought she wanted, what she thought would make her happy forever, only to discover yet again that it was less than she had hoped. John was a beautiful man but that, alas, was all he was. He was just a handsome outline that she had spent months grafting details onto. Instead of the lover she imagined, he was a real person and not an especially likeable one. He had to leave. Now.

Sara walked into the living room, climbed onto a chair, found the test button for the smoke alarm and pressed it for all she was worth.

Two circuits down, two to go. Four hills down, four to go. As they exited town, with 20 miles under their belt and 20 still ahead, Max was racking his brains. He had been cagey, hanging back, letting others do the work. He couldn't beat them with his strength and speed. He had to beat them with his brains. This was about wisdom over youth, age over beauty.

So what the fuck should he do?

If he continued to hang back, he was going to get dropped on one of the hills. That was pretty evident. Yes, so far, he had pulled himself back into contention by the top of each hill. But he was tiring. If he started at the back of the pack when they hit the final four climbs, there was a good chance he'd eventually be left behind, probably sooner rather than later. He couldn't afford to conserve his energy any longer.

Two-and-a-half miles into the third circuit, and with the next hill looming, Max pulled out of the pace line and sprinted to the front. Other riders turned to look. Somebody else pulled out of the pace line and tried to grab his back wheel. As Max passed, the cyclist at the front of the pace line sat up, bewildered, and started to freewheel. The pace line disintegrated, cyclists grabbing their brakes and pulling out to the left and right.

Max hit the hill, climbed out of the saddle and tried to power his way up. His quads didn't scream, which was a plus, but his speed was hardly impressive. The bike computer told a dreary tale: 20 mph, 18, 17, 15, 11. Max dug deep and drove the speed back up to 12. He was still at the front and he knew those behind were scrambling to catch up.

One rider passed and Max's heart sank. Then another passed. Then a third. But that was where the carnage ended. To his astonishment, Max reached the top of the hill in fourth place. He looked back briefly, saw riders scattered across the hill, and threw in a brief acceleration to catch the wheel in front of him.

The break was on. One other rider latched on and together the front five tore down the road. Behind them, the remains of the pack tried to organize, but it was too late. Most of the riders were too shot to form an effective chase group. Their day was done.

Max took a brief pull at the front and then drifted back, grabbing the end of the pace line and settling into the draft. They were flying along at 25, 26 mph. Think, he exhorted himself, think.

But the effort and the oxygen deprivation were taking their toll, and Max wasn't thinking too clearly. Forget grand strategy. How would he survive the next hill? The key, he figured, was once again to be at the front of the pack, so he had ground to cede as they headed skyward.

He got lucky. He managed to time it so he was on the front as they approached the circuit's second hill. He pressed the pace, keeping the speed close to 26 mph as they hit the bottom of the hill. They were barely into the climb when a rider came by and then a second one. But that was it. Max's eyes locked onto the second rider's back wheel and he imagined himself surgically attached. He measured his effort, doing all that was necessary to stay on the wheel in front of him and nothing more. They hit the top of the hill. Max was surprised to find they were alone. Two more riders had been dropped. The lead group was now just three.

Clare watched her father fly through town, just him and two other riders. She was shocked. She thought he would finish in the top 20—maybe. But she also saw the suffering in his face. She could see the sweat. He appeared fragile, slight, certainly older and smaller than the other two riders. It seemed unfair. The other two were so much younger, their thighs so much more muscular, as though they could crush her father at any moment.

The trio disappeared into the distance and a motley crew of cyclists followed, some alone, some in twos and threes. Clare turned her attention to the row of shops. She headed to a café in search of more coffee.

She was a maelstrom of conflicting emotions. She felt protective toward her father. But she also expected him to protect her. She disapproved of how he had behaved. But she also wanted his approval.

What was with the affair? It seemed so tacky, such a cliché, a middle-aged man losing interest in his wife of 25 years and sneaking around with another woman. It had devastated the family. Her mother couldn't even bring herself to talk about it. Clare phoned often, but her mother rarely called her back.

Clare never imagined her father was the sort of person who would have an affair. She thought him better than that. For all the turmoil it created, it wasn't even much of an affair: After her mother had tossed him out, it only lasted a handful of weeks. She had been so proud of her father, revering him as the cornerstone of their family's security and stability, the one person she could always count on. But now she wondered whether he was worthy of such pride. Was this all part of the mortality crisis they joked about so often?

Was this also the reason for the bicycling? Was it some last hurrah? Why couldn't he age gracefully like her other friends' parents? Why would he want to compete in a bike race? It was like an old guy dressing in a teenager's clothes, adopting the latest slang and pretending to be young and cool. It was unseemly. He didn't belong in this race. He was clearly outgunned. Her Dad might finish in the top three. But he sure wasn't going to win.

Top three. Max relished the prospect. Against these younger, stronger riders, a top-three finish would be a triumph.

Before the race, he'd tried to tamp down his expectations, tried to convince himself that where he placed didn't matter, that what counted was some vague sense that he had given it his all. But here he was, neck-and-neck with a couple of kids who might be 20 or 25 years younger, competing for a spot in the top three. Could he hang on? Could he do better than third?

They were halfway through the final circuit. Ahead lay five miles and one last hill. Max and the other two riders were working well together, taking turns at the front pulling their truncated train toward the finish line. If this was a pro race or even a half-decent amateur race, the riders behind would form a chase group and their speeding pace line would quickly catch the front three riders. But based on his glimpse from the top of the last hill, Max doubted it would happen. He hadn't seen anybody. He assumed those behind them were in disarray. The three leading riders wouldn't be caught.

Max pulled off the front and tucked in behind the second rider. His thinking was befuddled and his legs were growing heavy with the effort. What should he do? What was the right strategy? He was suffering. His inclination was to think the others were fine, looking so confident and professional with their high-end bikes and their slick riding shirts and shorts. But were they really fine? They must be suffering also. One rider seemed pretty strong, especially on the climbs. The other appeared somewhat weaker. If Max tried to break away, how effectively would the other two work together?

But he knew he couldn't break away. His legs were too tired. He calculated the effort needed to get from here to the finish line. At the current bruising pace, he had barely enough in the tank to complete the distance, let alone accelerate away from the others and pull out a solo victory. His two competitors would catch him on the final climb. And if he did try to break away, there was a risk he would blow up and take that sharp descent into hell. His legs spent and his energy waning, he might be rapidly reduced to a puttering weekend cyclist. That wouldn't just be humiliating. Worse still, he might get caught by one of the riders behind and finish out of the top three.

So what was the right strategy? Max found it hard to concentrate. What should he do? Third would be great. But once he knew he had third wrapped up, why not go for the win? To have a chance, he needed to conserve his energy until closer to the finish. On his next turn at the front, he counted to ten and pulled off.

"Hey," the cyclist behind him shouted angrily.

"I'm cooked," Max gasped, playing it for all he was worth. "Too fucking old for this."

He slipped in behind the second rider and waited for the consequences. Would the other two shorten the pulls they took at the front? Max detected a slight slackening in their effort, but it wasn't much.

When he next got to the front, he pulled for 20, but bobbed up and down on the bike, like he was struggling, and then hung his head as he ceded the lead to the next rider. It was shameful. But Max didn't feel any shame. He couldn't outride these guys. But maybe he could outsmart them.

At mile 38, they started the final climb. The stronger rider rocketed up the hill. The weaker one tried to follow but soon slipped back. But he didn't slip back as much as Max. The gap widened and Max once again tried to control his panic. Breathe, he screamed at himself, breathe. Spin the pedals. Spin the pedals. Keep the cadence high. Pull yourself back. "Please," he begged the bicycle.

The gap held steady for a while and then started to close, but Max still crested the hill 30 feet behind the other two. He shifted into a harder gear, stood up on the pedals and drove himself over the top of the hill and into the descent that followed. He sat down, continuing to shift into higher and higher gears. He drew a bead on the back wheel of the second rider, lined himself up and went into a tuck, his backside pushed off the back of the saddle, his chin on the handlebars, his elbows close to his chest, his knees locked either side of the frame, his feet at three and nine o'clock.

As his bike was dragged into the slipstream of the cyclists in front, Max hurtled ever closer, his speed climbing to 40, 45 and then briefly touching 47 mph. Like a slingshot, he flew past the other two riders and barreled on down the hill, still in the tuck position and milking everything he could out of his momentum. As the downhill started to flatten out, the other two riders came up behind Max. He continued to freewheel until they passed in frustration, at which point Max jumped onto the back of the train.

It was a little over a mile to go, not even three minutes of cycling. When would the others sprint? With 30 seconds to go? Maybe 40 seconds?

They entered Main Street for the final time. As they approached the center of town, newer homes gave way to grand Victorians with wide porches. Gnarly old trees shrouded the street, playing parent to the parking meters below. Max saw the finishing banner in the distance. He couldn't outsprint the stronger rider. Let's face it, he probably couldn't outsprint the weaker rider.

But what if he lengthened the sprint, so it was more of a long drive to the finish line? Could he come around and pass the two other riders without them latching onto his back wheel and taking advantage of the draft? Could he hammer all the way to the finish line from this far out? Did he have enough left in his legs?

Max realized he didn't have much choice. It was the only strategy that would give him a shot at victory. He filled his lungs with air, rose up out of the saddle, swung the bike hard to the right, pointed it toward the finish line, dipped his head, closed his eyes and powered the pedals with all his might.

Clare saw Max rise out of the seat. He was her 48-year-old father and yet, at that moment, he was somebody else entirely. The muscles in his arms were taut. His face and legs glistened with perspiration. As the bike leapt forward and gathered speed, he sat down, shifted into an easier gear and spun the pedals with a controlled fury. For a few brief seconds, the beauty was unmistakable.

Max's bike hurtled past the other two riders. A yawning gap immediately opened up. Max had his chance. He had broken free of the other two, who were now belatedly trying to respond, their suddenly feverish motion signaling how surprised they were. Max was 80 excruciating seconds from the finish line.

And then, like an old movie reel that's malfunctioning, the picture turned jerky, everything stalling out before the film leapt forward once again. Clare watched as Max's front wheel dipped into the slatted metal grill covering a roadside drain. The front wheel stopped with a jarring finality. But the back wheel kept going, twisting to the left with a violence that captivated the crowd. The brute force wrenched the front wheel from the metal grill and the bicycle continued down the road sideways, Max still hunched over the handlebars, his body angled forward and leading the charge, while the two wheels lagged behind.

As the bike clattered to the ground, she watched her father's left shoulder smash into the asphalt. Max and the bicycle took one sickening bounce, his body careering upward and onward, and then he skidded to a halt, his helmet running along the road and his head shoved down toward his chest.

For a brief moment, all was silent. Then people started to run.

Melanie sat in her dorm room, eyeing the pile of textbooks. She was slightly hung over from the night before. Why had she gone to that stupid party at the fraternity? During her freshman year, she couldn't wait for Friday and Saturday evenings and the parties at the frats. But now that she was a senior, the whole scene seemed totally lame, a noxious mix of booming music, cheap beer and stale sweat. Guys would try to chat her up, but she couldn't hear anything they said, so the conversation deteriorated into a third-rate game of charades.

She had broken up with her boyfriend eight months ago. She wasn't sure why. It just seemed like too much work and she was fairly confident the relationship was going nowhere. Besides, she was sick of him trying to paw her. There was no way she was sleeping with him.

Many of her friends were living off campus, but she had opted for campus housing, so she didn't have to walk so far to classes and the library. Despite a carefully cultivated image of academic sloth, her grades had been pretty decent through her freshman, sophomore and junior years, and she didn't want to risk slipping in her final year. But was that the real reason she had chosen to live on campus, rather than off campus with her friends? Her head ached, she had a shitload of work to do and she felt lonely.

How had she ended up so isolated? Had she done this to herself? Yeah, maybe she had. It was the image she was trying to project: cool aloof girl, black clothing, multiple ear piercings, hair dyed jet black, sort of Goth. But it was only meant to be an image. She didn't really want to be alone. Her best times were when she was hanging out with friends, drinking coffee, chatting about their courses and gossiping about pretty much anybody.

It wasn't just her friends that she was estranged

from. She hadn't bothered to go home over the summer, instead staying on in Chicago for a supposedly great internship. In truth, there was no internship. She had worked as a waitress, and spent most of the summer bored out of her mind and missing her family.

Even so, Melanie rarely called home these days. She didn't want to get caught in the shit-storm between her parents. It was also a fun little power play. If she didn't phone, her parents would always call her. Give them ten days without a call or an email and they would be on the phone, trying to sound blasé but obviously anxious to check she was okay. They were so predictable. Melanie found it amusing. She knew she was being a bit of an asshole. But she figured there would be time to patch things up later.

Her cell phone rang. She glanced at the small screen. It was her sister. "Hey, Clare."

"Hey, Mel." Clare's voice was hoarse and low. "I've got bad news. I'm here at the bike race. Dad's had an accident."

He watched the lights above him flash past as he turned tight corners and finally came to a halt. It brought back memories of lying on the backseat of his parents' car at night, the highway lights whizzing by.

"We just need to wait here until the x-ray technician finishes with another patient," said the orderly who was wheeling Max around the emergency room.

"This is a strange way to see the world." Max was still staring at the ceiling. "You should try it sometime."

"You seem awfully cheery for somebody who is all busted up."

"What're you going to do?"

"You could talk about how much you hurt."

"Not sure what they gave me. But I'm not feeling too much pain."

"Probably just as well."

"Why? Because I look like crap?"

"Your face is a little messed up, but some stitches should fix that. You've got a few dislocated fingers. They said you broke your left shoulder blade. Scapula, they call it. The doctors were impressed. Those things are tough to break. They said something about a motorcycle accident."

"Not a motorcycle. A bicycle."

"What happened? Were you hit by a car?"

"No, I did it all by myself. In a bicycle race."

"Impressive."

"If I hadn't crashed, I might have won."

"Shame."

"Or, at least, finished in the top three."

"Still a shame."

"Yeah, it is, it really is. But you know what? It'll still make a hell of a story for the grandkids."

Clare sat next to Max's bed in the emergency room. The curtains were drawn around them, but they could hear the hushed conversations from the other beds. There was an odd camaraderie, all these strangers thrown together by misfortune and sharing in each other's pain.

"How's the bicycle?"

"Strange to relate, I didn't spend a lot of time examining the bike. It looked like the handlebars and the seat were a little twisted around, but there may be other damage. The local police took it. They said we should call before we come to pick it up."

"I hope she's okay. I feel terrible about what happened."

"Dad, you're an idiot. If you haven't noticed, you're the one who needed the ambulance ride."

"But the frame might be cracked. The rear derailleur could be bent."

"Sweet Jesus, you'd think you and the stupid bike were having some great love affair."

Max was stumped for a response.

"Melanie is flying in," continued Clare, her eyes a mixture of concern and affection.

"You're kidding?"

"When I told her about the accident, she was super-upset."

"Wow, I'm surprised."

"That's two of us." They both chuckled, then Clare turned serious. "You can't go back to that horrible apartment."

"Why not? I can take care of myself."

"The evidence suggests otherwise. You look awful and you can barely sit up on your own. You were briefly unconscious. You shouldn't be alone if you're concussed." Clare examined her father, dried blood on his face, his fingers twisted, his left shoulder unnaturally still. "You could ask Mom to take you back."

"No, I can't."

"I think she misses you. I called her. She sounded really concerned. She knows that other woman broke up with you."

"I can't go back. That would be settling. I tried that before. Can't do it."

"So what are you going to do? Ride around on your bike all day with a broken shoulder blade?"

"Maybe. Or maybe something else. I've been trying to figure it out. I ran the numbers a few weeks ago. I have just about enough money so I don't have to work. Maybe I'll start another financial advisory business. I've thought about it. Or maybe I'll retire and find something completely different to do, something new, something I'll be passionate about, something that'll give more meaning to my days."

"Like what?"

"I don't know," said Max, shaking his head sadly. "I really don't know. I've given it a lot of thought and I keep drawing a blank. It's almost like I have too much choice. That's the problem with having money. It gives you so many options and it's hard to decide which is the right one. But you've got to keep looking, keep moving, find something that excites you."

Clare gave him a worried look. "Maybe you're spending too much time alone, Dad."

"Yeah, probably. I've lately had all these thoughts rattling around in my head. Problem is, I know how the whole thing plays out. I'll find something I want to do and initially it'll be exciting and challenging, like work used to be when I was your age. But after a while, the excitement will fade and I'll feel vaguely dissatisfied, so I'll try something else. And on and on and on. We just aren't very good at figuring out what will make us happy, maybe because we focus on the wrong thing. The real satisfaction isn't in achieving our goals. It's in the striving. That's the fun part, the really satisfying part. I don't know whether it's something truly transcendent or it's just some basic survival instinct. But it's when I'm striving that I feel most alive. Like I felt today."

"Like when you almost died."

"That was unfortunate," Max allowed. "But it was pretty damn exhilarating up until that point. If you'd ask me before the race, I would have told you that winning would be the thrill of a lifetime. But the truth is, the thrill probably would have faded pretty quickly."

"It's a shame you didn't think about that before you sprinted like a madman past those other two riders and crashed your bike."

"You're a cruel child. Have I mentioned that before?"

"Many times."

"I think you get it from your mother's side of the family. Anyway, seriously, I don't think winning would have made me happy for long. I think there would have been some nagging sense of disappointment, that it wasn't as life-transforming as I imagined. It's almost better that I didn't get what I wanted. Instead, it was the run-up to the race that was the really fun part, all the miles on the bike, learning about cycling, getting myself back into shape, pushing myself to go faster and faster. It just wasn't fun in the conventional sense. It was the struggle and truly being in the moment and squeezing everything you can out of yourself. Despite all the bad stuff that's happened over the past six months—breaking up with your mother, losing the business, today's accident—it's been years since I've been this excited by my life."

"You're a sick man, Dad. Maybe you hit your head too hard. You make happiness sound exhausting and painful and ultimately unsatisfying."

"What can I say? I think that's the way it is. It's the pursuit of happiness that's the fun part, the really satisfying part, but we always come up short in the end. Even when we get what we think we want, it's never as exhilarating as we imagine. The pleasure just doesn't last all that long. Despite a lifetime of effort, despite all our striving, none of us ends our lives standing on the winner's podium, arms raised in triumph, happy and satisfied with all that we've achieved."

Then Max gave Clare a pained smile.

He walked into the old deli, his left arm in a sling and his dislocated fingers taped together. The swelling in his face had largely subsided, and the cuts and stitches were covered by eight days of beard growth. His legs were fine and he tried to put forth a confident stride, but his discomfort was evident to anyone who looked closely. He kept his upper body as still as possible, trying to avoid the sudden movements that would cause his fractured shoulder to scream.

Max had been feeling antsy from lack of exercise, so he settled on a walk to his old lunchtime haunt. Along the way, he passed the offices of Whitfield Financial Advisors. A "For Rent" sign hung in the window. An old client told him Alison needed to slash overhead, so she was ditching the offices and planned to run the business out of her apartment. If anything, that made matters worse. The client sensed financial trouble and had pulled his account. He said others were also defecting.

Max had mixed feelings. Whatever pleasure he felt at Alison's comeuppance was more than offset by his distress at seeing his life's work collapse. Whitfield Financial had been his baby. Soon, it would be no more. He had thought briefly about trying to buy back the remains of the business from Alison. But he still wasn't sure he wanted to return to the advisory business and, if he did, he figured reclaiming the helm of Whitfield Financial would trigger all kinds of bad memories. It would be more fun to start from scratch.

The counter staff greeted him like he was still a regular: There was no small talk, just undisguised impatience. "Next," came the summons.

"Italian sub, lettuce and tomato, oil and vinegar. And go ahead, throw some onions on there."

"Brave man."

Max turned to face an attractive woman. He knew her. He knew that he knew her. Goddamn it, how did he know her?

"Remember me?"

Fuck. Double fuck. Max tried to hide his panic, smiled noncommittally and scanned her face, immediately drawn to the birthmark above her lip.

"I took your advice," she said.

And then it twigged. "Let me guess," said Max, ripping the memory from some long abandoned corner of his mind. She was the woman he had tried to chat up back in the spring. "You started reading trashy novels."

"I did."

"So how's that working for you?"

"I like them. They always have happy endings. It's

totally unrealistic. But it cheers me up and keeps me going." She eyed Max's battered face. "So what happened to you?"

"I lost my wife, I lost my lover, I lost my business and I lost control of my bike."

She looked startled by his honesty. "That doesn't sound good."

"Actually, it's okay. We humans are remarkably resilient. Just as pleasure seems to be fleeting, so does pain. Bad things happen and we think they're a terrible tragedy, but then we get over them surprisingly quickly. I think it will turn out okay. I know I'm probably totally delusional, but I'm also hoping for a happy ending. By the way, I'm Max."

"I remember. After that first time, I kept thinking I'd see you here again, but I never did. I'm Beth."

"Delighted to meet you, Beth, presumably with an 'h'."

"Huh?"

"It's a long story. Would you like to hear it? We could have lunch. I know this great Italian deli."

ABOUT THE AUTHOR

Jonathan Clements is the former personal-finance columnist for *The Wall Street Journal*. He was born in London, England, graduated from Emmanuel College, Cambridge University, and now lives in New York City. He wrote for *Euromoney* magazine in London and *Forbes* magazine in New York before joining the *Journal*, where he worked for 18 years. While *48 and Counting* is his first novel, Jonathan has written four earlier books, the latest of which is *The Little Book of Main Street Money: 21 Simple Truths that Help Real People Make Real Money*, published by John Wiley & Sons in 2009. For additional information, head to www.jonathanclements.com.

17676733R00087

Made in the USA
Lexington, KY
27 September 2012